Deidra's Last Dance

By

Wm. Sharpe

Edited by

James R. Sodon

Edited by James R. Sodon

Cover design by M. Thomas

ISBN: 9798849482880

Published 2022 by
BearhounD7 ProductionS LLC
Saint Louis, Missouri
BearhounD7ProductionS.com
Available from Amazon.com and other stores

Deidra's Last Dance
Is
Dedicated
To
Juanita Scherer

Devoted Wife and Mother

Grandmother and Mother-in-Law

Sister-in Law

Kind and Generous Friend

Loyal Supporter and Reader

Book Reviewer and Critic

Nick Caldwell's #1 Fan

Thank You

W.S.

2022

Dedication

For my wife, Linda

For my daughter Sondra, I love you and miss you

For James R. Sodon, my friend, editor and conscience

For Eric Eggemeyer and Elise Eggemeyer, my "kids"

For Kenneth "The Neth" Harrison, my friend and favorite
poet, cartoonist and composer, you are missed

For Drew Foster, my friend and a dreamer, you are missed

For Pam

How do you say goodbye to a friend, a gatekeeper, a confidant, a big sister, one who protected you from those who would do you harm and one who protected you from yourself at times? How do you say goodbye to someone who knew and understood, with almost a sixth sense, who was ethical and honest and who was not? How do you say goodbye to someone whose only flaw was that their sense of humor was similar to yours?

The answer is you don't. You feel the loss, you shed a tear because you will miss that they are not there, but you don't say goodbye. You say farewell and if you believe in something bigger than yourself, you say, "See you on the other side," and you smile, remembering your friend.

WS
August 2020

Thank you to

The Ladies of Edit Ink:
Karen Eggemeyer
and Linda Eggemeyer-Sharpe

Baron, Ruby, Tink and Sheiky
our family's best friends
who always make me smile

Chapter 1

Nick rolled over in bed and looked at the clock on the bed stand. Why is it the phone always seems louder when it rings in the middle of the night?

"Hello, this better be good," he growled into the phone.

"Nick, it's Sinclair, I can't sleep."

"So you thought it would be a good idea to call me so I can't sleep?" Nick asked. "Didn't I put you on a plane for New Orleans about six hours ago?"

"I've been thinking," Sinclair said.

"Obviously not very well if you thought it was a good idea to call me at this hour. You woke up Baron and Ruby," Nick said.

"Nick, I need your help," Sinclair said. "It's important."

"What's so important that it couldn't wait until morning?"

"I need you to come down here," Sinclair said.

"To New Orleans?" Nick asked. "When?"

"I need you to get a morning flight and bring Phil," Sinclair said.

There was something in his voice that Nick had never heard before: it was a mixture of concern and fear. He had never known Sinclair to be afraid of anything.

"What's going on?" Nick asked.

"I'm afraid I may kill someone," Sinclair said.

"You're going to kill somebody?" Nick asked. "Who for God's sake?"

"The man that killed my daughter," Sinclair said, without emotion.

"The man who killed your daughter, thirty-five years ago," Nick said.

"Yes," Sinclair said.

"You know who killed your daughter?" Nick asked.

"Yes," Sinclair said.

1

"You have any facts, evidence or proof to back this up?" Nick asked.

"I will, but I am afraid when I lay eyes on him, I will kill him," Sinclair said.

"What do you have to go on? You didn't mention you had a lead before you left," Nick said.

"I didn't have a lead until I got back tonight," Sinclair said.

"Sinclair, I'm worried," Nick said. "What do you have?"

"Nick, I have a hunch," Sinclair said.

Nick was silent for a moment.

Sinclair Stewart, maybe the best detective Nick had ever known, never had hunches. He was tireless when looking for evidence. He didn't shoot from the hip on cases. He was a very serious man when it came to his investigations.

"Nick, can you and Phil come down?" he asked.

"We'll be on the first flight we can get," Nick said.

"Thank you. When you get in, come to the house; you can stay here," Sinclair said.

"We'll call you before we get on the plane," Nick said.

"Thanks again," Sinclair said and hung up.

Nick was wide awake. He walked downstairs, made coffee, and called his brother Phil.

Phil answered, "You need to be bailed out or did someone shoot you again?"

"Sinclair may be in trouble, he called, I'm worried," Nick blurted out. "We're going to New Orleans this morning. I have to call Bart and let him know. Can you call Katie and ask if she can come over here and take care of Baron and Ruby?"

"Sure," Phil said.

"I'll call and make the reservations and call you back with the flight and time," Nick said.

"What's all this about?" Phil asked.

"We'll talk on the plane."

"Okay, you want me to come over or are you going to pick me up?" Phil asked.

2

"I'll pick you up," Nick said.

"See you then," Phil said.

Nick hung up and looked at Baron and Ruby. They were lying on the couch after following him downstairs.

Nick looked at them and said, "Your buddy, Sinclair, has a hunch."

Baron raised his head and looked at Nick with almost a puzzled expression, as if he were thinking, Sinclair doesn't do hunches. Then he laid his head down and in a minute or two began to snore.

Chapter 2

Nick arrived at seven at Phil's apartment. He was dressed, packed and ready to go.

"Do you have any idea why we're making this trip? He was up here for Christmas, was here through New Year's and left yesterday," Phil said. "So, again, do you know why we are making this trip?"

"Yes," Nick said, then was silent.

"Well?" Phil asked.

"He thinks he knows who killed his daughter," Nick said.

"He found a lead?" Phil asked.

"Nope, he has a hunch," Nick said.

"A hunch, Sinclair has never had a hunch in his life. He is intuitive, but he has never had a 'hunch' that was not backed up by evidence and fact. A hunch is like those things that hack reporters get, like that Acosta guy on CNN, not veteran investigators like Sinclair Stewart."

"Well, he says he has one," Nick said, "and we're going to hear him out."

There was silence in the car and as they went through the check in.

Phil was amused watching eighty-year-old grandmas being shaken down and having their wheelchairs searched for explosives and their ISIS membership cards.

When they boarded the plane, they lucked out. Nick got his isle seat, Phil got the window, and there was no one in the middle seat.

When they were settled and in the air, Phil said, "You know, I noticed that Sinclair wasn't himself after Dad's Christmas Eve party."

"What do you mean?" Nick asked.

"He was a little distant and subdued on New Year's Eve," Phil said.

4

"He's never been one to put a lamp shade on his head on New Year's," Nick replied.

"I'm just saying the week after Christmas he spent a lot of time talking with Dad and Dalton," Phil said, "and he also spent time with Katie, Maeve and little Bridget."

"Well, Dalton and Dad are old cops," Nick said, "and they like to swap stories. And if he has been thinking about his daughter's case, it probably makes him feel good to be around Katie, Maeve and Bridget, thinking about what his daughter may have been at that age."

"Do you do that?" Phil asked.

"Do what?" Nick said.

"Think about Mary and what she might be like if she..." Phil stopped.

"If some dirt bags who were trying to off me hadn't killed her by mistake?"

Phil did not reply.

"Every damned day," Nick said.

Phil looked out the window and wished he hadn't said a damned thing. There was an awkward silence.

Phil clumsily changed the subject. "Did you hear anything from Dad about what he may be planning to do?"

Nick looked at him and smiled. "Nope, Billy doesn't confide in me. After all, I'm son number two. I did hear what he was planning from son number one."

"He told Wil?" Phil asked.

"Of course," Nick said, with a laugh.

"Why doesn't he ever tell us anything?" Phil asked, almost feigning a pout.

"You know why," Nick said. "Wil is number one son, and a detective and member in good standing with the Chicago Police Department, and we are just vagabond gumshoes without discipline or a good sense of duty. We're not true blue; we are renegades that get in the way of real law enforcement."

"But we're nice people," Phil said.

Nick looked at him.

5

"Well, I'm a nice person," Phil said, with a smile. "He tells Laura things and she's a detective too."

"Yes, but our sister is the baby and more importantly, she has given him two grandchildren. Wil and you have not. And I have lost my children and somehow I think he still blames me," Nick said.

"I could still give him grandchildren," Phil said.

"Yeah?" Nick asked. "Who are you dating now? Besides, he doesn't like you telling people you got the same score on psych tests that Gacy and Bundy got."

"It's a joke," Phil said.

"Billy doesn't do jokes," Nick said.

"What did Wil tell you?" Phil asked.

"Billy is moving down around where Dalton is so he can fish, drink and sit around at dinner and tell cop stories," Nick said.

"He's moving to Caldwell?" Phil asked.

"Yep, he has found a cabin on the lake he's going to buy and live a life of leisure," Nick said.

"Isn't that what he has been doing since he retired from the Chicago cop shop?" Phil asked.

"Yeah, but he has become disenchanted with Chicago. He constantly reminds us that what is wrong with Chicago is that it was dumb enough to elect a mayor who went to school where I went," Nick said.

"She went to Loyola?" Phil asked.

"No, Michigan," Nick said, "and has no respect for the police, the law, or the people of Chicago."

"I can think of a lot more reasons than that not to like what's going on," Phil said.

"Me too, but with Billy, I think that the mayor and I went to the same school may be the primary reason he doesn't like her," Nick said.

They both laughed.

"What's he going to do with the house?" Phil asked.

"I thought he'd offer it to Wil, but it looks like Laura and Bob are moving to Chicago. We are all going to be talking about that at the annual meeting," Nick said. "The St. Louis office has lost a lot of personnel and they haven't developed the corporate clients that were expected. So, we are going to close or downsize it, and Bob and Laura and anyone else that wants to can come to the Chicago office. Bart has brought in more clients than expected."

We're really going to close down St. Louis?" Phil asked. "I liked that office."

"It's not final, but it might be the smart thing to do," Nick said. "I trust what Bart is doing. He loves the corporate side of the business, and he is great at it. As you know, I've never been that excited about it, but it has made us very profitable."

"Are there any other surprises," Phil asked.

Nick smiled and said, "There are always surprises."

They arrived in New Orleans around noon, rented a car, and headed toward the Stewart homestead near the Quarter.

Chapter 3

As the they approached the home of Sinclair Stewart, Phil looked at the tall old wooden wall and gate and was surprised.

Nick noticed and asked, "What's wrong?"

"Nothing," Phil said, "I just, well I guess, I expected..."

Nick cut him off, "More?"

"Yes," Phil answered.

Nick parked the car by the wall. There was a door in the wall that you could miss if you didn't know where to look. Behind the wall large oak trees towered above the wall and there was a hint of magnolia in the air.

If one looked closely enough at those old oaks, they would notice a series of lights and cameras mounted and blending into the branches of the trees.

Near the almost invisible door was a nearly invisible button.

Nick pushed the button and the nearly invisible door opened. Nick and Phil walked through. For Phil it was like the first time he saw the *Wizard of Oz*, at the moment Dorothy traveled from Kansas and landed in Oz.

They walked into a garden and the entry to a town home. Indeed, there were oak trees, there were also many other flowering plants, and a small lawn with bushes. On the many balconies there were hanging plants. On one side of the courtyard was the home and garage, the rest looked like a smaller version of a botanical garden in a large city.

"I'm in here," they heard Sinclair say. There was a cast iron fence with hanging Jasmine around a small patio area where two French doors were open leading into the house.

They walked through the doors and Sinclair was sitting behind a large, polished Regency Scottish Mahogany 6-Drawer Partners Writing Table. Behind the desk were two portraits, one of Sinclair's late wife and one of his murdered daughter.

Sinclair was smoking a Peterson pipe with a glass of bourbon in his hand. "Thanks for coming," he said, "sit down." They sat in two high back chairs. "You want a drink?"

"A little early for me, but thank you," Nick said.

They sat and looked at each other.

"Kill anyone this morning," Nick asked.

"Not yet," Sinclair said, "but the day is early."

Phil, like most of the young detectives that had worked cases with Sinclair was not completely sure that he was not serious.

"What's going on here?" Nick asked.

"I know who killed my little girl. I told you that," Sinclair said.

"Okay, who do think killed her?" Nick said.

"I don't think, I know he did," Sinclair replied.

"How do you know," Nick said.

"I know," Sinclair said.

"Do you have evidence," Nick asked.

"I will," he said.

"You will?" Nick said.

"Damn it, I said I will," he blurted.

"Do you have a motive for why he did what he did?" Nick asked.

"Nick, you can say 'kill her.' I am fully aware what happened to her thirty-five years ago," he said.

"Let's start from the beginning. How did you get this information?" Nick asked.

"It came to me. I just know," Sinclair said, with more than a hint of irritation.

"Did you get a tip or find something that pointed you in a direction or something that you overlooked? Sinclair, you don't have hunches. You are a very methodical man. How did you know who did this? This doesn't make sense," Nick said.

"I just know," he repeated.

"We can't investigate unless you give us something to investigate,' Nick said, "so what is your proof?"

"I don't need proof, I know," Sinclair said.

"That is not good enough and you know it," Nick said. "You have said yourself, 'knowing is one thing but proving is another.' You want to bring this guy to justice, you have to prove he is guilty."

"I don't have to prove anything. I just have to put my hands around his neck and choke the truth out of him, then choke the life out of him to give him justice," Sinclair said.

Nick fired back, "That's not justice; you know that's revenge and it will land you in Angola and with the numbers you have sent there in your career, you wouldn't last long in there."

"Are you going to help me or not?" Sinclair asked.

"I will help investigate and find evidence and proof, but I won't help you go after someone without evidence of guilt," Nick said.

"He killed my child. Why won't you help?" Sinclair screamed.

"Because, what if you are wrong? What if your hunch is wrong? What if you 'give justice' to an innocent man?" Nick screamed back.

"I know he is guilty," Sinclair said.

"Then prove it!" Nick said.

There was a long silence.

"Do you even know the name of your suspect?" Nick asked.

"Yes," said Sinclair.

"Well, who is he?" Nick asked.

Sinclair hung his head and said, "Fontane Barbeau."

"Who the hell is Fontane Barbeau?" Nick asked.

"He has owned a dance studio for the last fifty years," Sinclair said.

"And this is relevant, why?" Nick asked.

"He was her dance instructor for eight years," he said.

"What makes you think he is the person who took her from you?" Nick asked.

Sinclair took a thick file from his desk. It was old and well read. He opened it and showed Nick and Phil the crime scene photos. Phil almost became ill. It was the picture of a very young girl on the verge of becoming an attractive young woman. She had been strangled.

Nick could feel a growing anger that took him back to when he had to view his own daughter's file. He steadied himself before he spoke. "What did you find in this file or see in these pictures that led you to believe that Barbeau did this?" Nick asked.

Sinclair, with a steady voice, said, "It's not what is here, it is what isn't here, what's missing," he said.

"What isn't here?" Phil asked.

"A locket," Sinclair said. "She never took it off from the time it was given to her."

"This still doesn't prove Barbeau is involved," Nick said.

"Her mother gave it to her not long before she passed. It was her most important treasure," he said

Nick said, "Still, it doesn't prove…"

Sinclair interrupted. "He has a little lock box hidden in the office of his studio. In that box we will find the locket my wife gave our daughter with her initials on it and inside the locket there is…"

"There is what?" Nick asked.

"A picture of her mother and me," Sinclair said. "There will also be other items of young girls that he has hurt."

Sinclair seemed almost in a trance.

"Listen, why don't you get some rest," Nick said. "We'll get dinner and get a good night's sleep and get an early start in the morning and go over the case file and talk about how we are going to investigate this case. Sinclair, you and I solved a case in St. Louis no one ever thought could be solved. Let's work the case."

Sinclair looked at him and said, "He did it, Nick, I'm sure."

Chapter 4

After eating dinner in, they sat around the parlor and talked about nothing in particular. They had agreed that they would start fresh in the morning. About ten thirty Phil was wiped out and tired of listening to Nick and Sinclair talk about police work, cases, and anything else that happened before he graduated from high school.

They finished off three-quarters of a bottle of Dewar's and called it a night. As Sinclair and Nick were walking up the stairs, Sinclair asked, "Do you think I should have told Phil about the ghosts who roam this house?"

"No," Nick said, "don't they say that discovery is half of the adventure."

They both laughed and retired to their respective rooms.

+

When Phil stumbled down the stairs, Nick and Sinclair were sitting in the dining room drinking coffee and having breakfast.

"Sleep well?" Sinclair asked as Phil yawned.

"No," he replied," I had the weirdest dreams and it felt like I was being watched."

"Really?" Sinclair said, looking at Nick.

"Maybe you were being watched," Nick said.

"By whom?" Phil asked.

"Could've been a number of people, but it was probably my great-great-great uncle, Brigadier General Jack MacGregor Stewart, who died from his wounds in that room in 1863," Sinclair said.

"You had a relative that was a general in the Civil War?" Phil asked.

"Not exactly," Sinclair said.

"What battle did he die in?" Phil asked.

"He didn't," Sinclair said.

"How did he die from his wounds," Phil asked.

"Well, 'Old General Jack' was made a U.S. Grant look-a-like, an A.A. member with a twenty-five-year coin of sobriety. He was on patrol not far from here and he fell asleep on his horse one night and the horse, who some said was as big a drunk as General Jack, trotted home.

When Jack arrived here, he woke up and after such a long ride had a great thirst. He knew his father had hidden barrels of whisky in the cellar. So Jack went to the cellar to liberate a bottle. It was dark in the cellar, so as he stumbled down the stairs to the cellar, he drew his sword. He fell, dropped the sword, and fell on it."

"He fell on his sword?" Phil asked.

"Yes, he did, and he wounded himself, but he was not going to be denied. He crawled until he found the whisky and grabbed a bottle and he picked up his sword and crawled back up the stairs, through this dining room into the hall and up the stairs to the room where you are staying with his sword in one hand and the bottle of whisky in the other. They found him the next morning with his sword in his right hand and the empty bottle in the other hand. He died a true credit to the Cause and the Confederacy. A good thing, too, because I have no doubt that had he lived, he would have been tried as a deserter and executed."

"Really?" Phil said.

"Son, a southern gentleman never lies--unless it is convenient. For one hundred fifty- eight years there have been stories that old General Jack roams the house still looking for another drink."

Nick smiled as he read the *Times-Picayune* and drank his coffee.

"Who knows, maybe you will get a chance to meet him while you're here," Nick said to Phil.

+

13

After breakfast they met in Sinclair's study.

"Sinclair, we need to run this like any other investigation of a cold case, agreed?"

"Agreed," Sinclair said, reluctantly.

"This morning, we start looking at the case files and any other information you have," Nick said.

Sinclair walked over to a closet and opened the door. Stacked four across, two deep and to the top of the closet were thirty-two banker boxes of files. Sinclair said, "There's more upstairs. I have been working this case a long time. There are also a few boxes in the office."

"Okay, let's start organizing the case files. It was a long time ago and we're going to want to interview anyone who was around back them. I'm sure a lot of the folks have passed on but if they are still around, we will need to talk to them. It is going to take us a while to get through the files.

"I think I will go to his studio this afternoon and look around. Is his studio in the same place?"

"Yes, but I think I should go too," Sinclair said.

"Not today," Nick.

"But," Sinclair objected.

"No buts. I don't want you to go all bad ass over this guy," Nick said. "Do you know anyone in the building department here?"

"You want the Land Records Division, it's on the seventh floor at City Hall," Sinclair said.

"How far would the records go back?" Nick asked.

"It was founded in 1827," Sinclair said.

"Good. Phil, go down there and see what information you can get on Barbeau's building. If they have plans get them. Tell them you are a grad student working on a historic building project," Nick said. "Also, research any other office that may have historic information about that area. Is Barbeau's building a historic building?"

"It should be," Sinclair said. It was probably built at the end of the war."

"Which war would that be?" Phil asked.

"For most of the folks down here there are only two wars that interest them, 1812 and 1860," Sinclair said. "I think his building was built at the end of the War of Northern Aggression." He laughed. "And sometimes I think that one is still being fought, Yankee."

"I'm from Chicago," Phil said.

"Sinclair, would you mind if I brought some folks down to help with the files?" Nick asked.

"We have plenty of room here, who do want to bring in?" Sinclair asked.

"I thought I would have Katie and Casey come in to work the files, Greg to look at any forensics that still might exist and Alana to work with Phil on some of the investigative work," Nick said.

"Fine by me," Sinclair said.

"Good. Phil, call Mrs. Marbles and see if she can round them up and get them down here," Nick said.

"I'll call now; they should all be in the office by now," Phil said.

"Okay, let's start looking at those files," Nick said.

Chapter 5

Nick stood in front of the four-story building with an attic on the edge of the French Quarter. It was probably built for small manufacturing, but for the last fifty years has served as dance studio for the "Paris of the South."

It had been kept up pretty well. On the front of the building a sign hung like a marque read:

Barbeau Dance Center
Established 1971
Ballet-Tap-Modern-Ballroom-Hip Hop-Folk
Fontane Barbeau
Founder & Artistic Director
Francois Barbeau
Instructor & Assistant Director
Antoine Barbeau
Instructor

Nick thought, what? No Irish or Scottish dance? He laughed and walked toward the building.

He entered a large reception area. There was a young woman sitting in what looked to be a box office. He walked up and said, "Excuse me."

"You're excused, "she said, with a smile. What may I do for you?"

There were so many answers to that question, he thought, but he said politely, "I would like to see Mr. Barbeau."

"Which one?" she asked, as she pointed to the wall behind the box office with a duplicate sign of the one on the front of the theatre.

Nick smiled his most charming smile. "Mr. Fontane Barbeau."

She did not return his most charming smile; she looked at him as if her tutu was in a knot. She wasn't actually wearing a tutu, but that was the first thing that popped into Nick's head.

"The Ballet Master is not in. May I ask what is the nature of your business with Monsieur Barbeau?"

Nick thought about saying he was there to ask if Monsieur Barbeau had been raping and killing any of the young women dancers in his school recently, but he thought better of it and said, "I am interested in historic buildings that had been redesigned for artistic uses over the last one hundred years." He gave another one of his most charming smiles.

"Are you some kind of professor?" the young woman asked.

"I am willing to enlighten and teach lessons to any who may need them," Nick replied, with his third most charming smile.

"Are you affiliated with a university?" she asked.

"I am. I lecture at Loyola University and the University of Michigan," Nick said with a slightly arrogant charming smile.

"At Loyola here in New Orleans?" she asked.

Nick thought that with all these questions, maybe he should hire this young women, but he said, "No, Loyola in Chicago and Michigan in Ann Arbor." This was not a lie; he did lecture at both schools in criminal investigation.

"Well, I am sorry you will have to make an appointment," she said.

"I will be in New Orleans for the next week or so. What would be convenient for Monsieur Barbeau?"

She looked at her appointment book, then looked up. "Monsieur Barbeau would be able to meet with you on Wednesday at ten. He will only have an hour, and he teaches a master class at eleven."

"That would be perfect," Nick answered, "Ten it is on Wednesday."

"Whom may I say he will be meeting with?" she asked.

"Nicholas Spencer Neff, at your service."

"What an unusual name," she said.

"Isn't it," Nick said with a charming smile. "Oh, here is my card, it has my number at both universities, and I will write the number I am staying at on the back."

+

Nick walked out of the building and walked down the street. When he could no longer be seen from the Barbeau school, he got his cell out and called Bart Cheswick, his partner and COO of Caldwell Investigations in Chicago.

Bart answered Immediately, "What's up Nick?"

"I used the alias card just a few minutes ago," Nick said.

"Which one?" Bart replied.

"The Nicholas Spencer Neff card. I am supposed to be an expert in historic buildings that had been redesigned for artistic uses over the last one hundred years," he said.

"You truly are a Renaissance man, aren't you?" Bart laughed. "What do you need?"

"You know the stash of cell phones with the different area codes that Mrs. Marbles has stashed away?" Nick asked.

"Yeah."

"Ask her to get a 312 and a 313 out and program the 312 with this message: 'Thank you for calling the Loyola University of Chicago School of History. Please leave a message and your call will be returned as soon as possible.' Get someone else to record the 313 with 'You have reached the University of Michigan School of Architecture and Design' with a similar message. Have someone look up the names of the administrative assistants for the deans of those departments. When Katie and Casey get down here, I will ask them to write a bio and script that can be used to vouch for Nicholas Spencer Neff."

"Anything else?" Bart asked.

"Yeah, I gave my most charming smile three times and the receptionist at the Barbeau School was not impressed. I am a little down," Nick said.

"I'm shocked," Bart said. "You didn't have her duct taped to a chair with a bright light in her face, did you?""

"Absolutely not, that may be Wednesday, and it will probably be her boss, Monsieur Barbeau," Nick said, with his most charming smile. "Bonne journée, Monsieur Bart."

Chapter 6

Sinclair was sitting in his office when Nick returned, He was smoking his pipe, looking through files.

"Did you get in to see the son of a bitch?" Sinclair asked.

"Nope, but I have an appointment for Wednesday at ten," Nick replied. "I told them I was interested in historic buildings that had been redesigned for artistic uses over the last one hundred years."

"They bought that?" Sinclair asked.

"Probably, but if they didn't, they have phone numbers to check up on me," Nick said.

"Don't tell me, you're using Mrs. Marbles' collection of burners with various area codes?" Sinclair asked, doing an imitation of a smokestack as the smoke from his pipe filled the office.

"Of course," Nick said. "Is Phil back yet?"

"No, but he called and said that Katie, Casey and Alana will get in this evening and Greg will be in tomorrow afternoon," Sinclair said. "I called Mrs. Sherman, my housekeeper, and their rooms will be ready later this afternoon. You can set up operations in the ballroom on the third floor."

Nick smiled.

"What's so funny," Sinclair asked.

"Housekeeper, ballroom, this is a side of you I've never seen." Nick laughed.

"What do you mean?" Sinclair asked.

"Sinclair Stewart, laird of the manor," Nick joked.

Sinclair blew a cloud of smoke and said, "Sinclair Stewart with size 12 boots, with one of those boots destined to be up your behind if you are not careful."

Nick laughed again. "Everyone likes a cranky senior citizen with a violent streak."

"Damn straight," Sinclair said, "you hungry?"

"I could eat," Nick said.

"Good. You know where the kitchen is, go fix something," Sinclair said.

"What, no cook?" Nick said. "I mean, I thought all plantation owners had a cook and a butler and..."

"Hey, block head have you noticed this house is in the city?" Sinclair said.

Nick smiled and took out his pipe, packed it with tobacco and lit it up.

"What kind of tobacco are you smoking?" Sinclair asked.

"Something better than that dried skunk and manure mix you're smoking," Nick said.

"It's better than that sissy blend you smoke," Sinclair countered.

"Hey, I bought this from Iwan & Ries in Chicago...the big city," Nick said.

"You bought it?" Sinclair said.

"I did," Nick replied.

"Really? I heard that when you moved the corporate office above Iwan & Ries, you cut a deal for free tobacco," Sinclair said.

"Who would spread such a vicious rumor?" Nick asked.

"Bart," Sinclair said. "You are the stereotype of the stingy Scotsman."

"I'm not stingy, I'm frugal," Nick said.

"You're cheap," Sinclair said, and for the first time since Nick and Phil arrived, he laughed.

"When did Phil say he would get back?" Nick asked.

"Before dinner," Sinclair said. "He's almost as cheap as you are."

"I doubt that, and I am not cheap, I am frugal." Nick laughed. "When he gets back, we have to go through the sequence of events of the case."

"Read the file," Sinclair said.

"I did," Nick said, "and now I need you to walk me through it."

"Do you know how hard that will be for me?" Sinclair said.

Nick looked at him.

"I'm sorry," Sinclair said. "I know you know."

"It was hard for me to go through Mary's case, but it was necessary," Nick said.

Sinclair looked at up Nick; it was the first time that he had seen any vulnerability in the old detective.

"How about you and I do it, without anyone else," Nick said, "just you and me and a bottle of bourbon."

Sinclair wiped his eyes and said, "Deal."

Both men sat in silence with swirls of smoke hovering over them.

Chapter 7

Around seven that evening there was a knock at the door. Sinclair answered the door and Nick could hear his delight at who was at the door. There were laughs and smiles. Sinclair was happy to see Casey, Katie, and Alana, even with all their luggage.

"How long you staying?" Sinclair asked.

"Until we catch the bad guy, Paw-Paw," Katie said. It was one of Sinclair's favorite sayings. Katie started calling Sinclair Paw-Paw, not long after she began calling Nick Pops. She had no family and was in and out of foster care as a kid, as was Greg, her childhood friend. Nick took an interest in them and now both work in the investigation field, Greg in forensics and Katie as an investigator. Nick's sister, Laura and her husband, Bob, also investigators and Nick's father, Billy, welcomed them into the Caldwell family.

Casey and Alana also worked for Caldwell Investigations, Casey in the St. Louis office and Alana in Chicago.

Casey, a few years older than the other two, was the big sister. She was the young Mrs. Marbles, which meant she was being groomed to the run the place, as Mrs. Marbles had done since Nick put his name on the door of the old Chicago offices above Blackie's. Mrs. Marbles claims to be retired and she makes that clear to anyone who comes to the office. She retired and went on vacation for two weeks. When she returned, she announced that she was retired but would be coming in everyday and most weekends. She insisted that Bart Cheswick, the COO of the firm, refer to her salary check as her pension. He did.

The three women were hovering around Sinclair, and he loved it.

Alana asked, "Where can we take our bags?"

I had the housekeeper open three rooms on the third floor. The girls looked tired.

Katie said, "Okay ladies, let's get those bags up and settle in."

"No need, I have someone who will take your bags up for you," Sinclair said with a smile. "Phillip, get your ass down here and help these beautiful young belles with their luggage," he yelled.

Phil came to the top of the stairs and said, "They look like healthy young women, and the exercise will be good for them."

"Chivalry is not dead in my home; get your butt down here...now!"

"Come on, Paw-Paw, I'm tired," Phil said as he walked downstairs.

Sinclair smiled and said, "Son, have you ever been shot?"

"No, you're thinking about Nick; he gets shot a lot," Phil replied.

"Do you want to get shot?" Sinclair asked.

Phil looked at him. "So, what rooms do these bags go in?"

"They have their choice of the rooms on the west wing," Sinclair said. "That would be on the opposite side of the hall where your room is."

As Phil struggled with the bags, Sinclair invited the ladies into the parlor. Nick followed them in.

"What do you want us to do first, Pops?" Katie asked.

Nick gave her the look, then began, "Greg is bringing the equipment in tomorrow. Sinclair wants us to set up in the ballroom on the second floor."

"Ballroom?" Alana said. "Cool, Paw-Paw."

"It's a small one," Sinclair said, with a smile.

"We will use it as our headquarters," Nick said. "We're going to need to get all the file boxes and crime files up there."

"We're going to have get all that equipment and the files up to the ballroom?" Casey asked.

"That's right," Nick said.

"Wow," Alana aid, "Greg and Phil are going to love that."

Sinclair said, "Don't worry, we can load up the elevator."

"You have an elevator?" Katie asked.

"Yes," Sinclair said, "it's located just off the kitchen, it goes from the cellar to the attic with stops on the main floor second floor and third floor."

Casey smiled. "And Phil doesn't know about it?"

"Nick, you didn't tell him about the elevator?" Sinclair said, feigning surprise.

"I guess I forgot," Nick said, smirking.

"You two are evil," Alana said, laughing.

"Did you get the message about the background script?" Nick asked.

"Yes, you're using the Neff ID?" Casey asked.

"Correct," Nick said.

"We worked on it on the plane, so it will be ready this evening,' Casey said.

"You want Alana and me to go undercover and take dance lessons?" Katie asked.

"No," Nick said, firmly.

"Hey, we were great the last time we went undercover," Alana said.

"You were," Nick said, "but the answer is still no."

"What do you want us to do tonight?" Casey asked.

Sinclair piped up. "I hoped that you all would be my guests at Pat O'Brien's this evening."

"The Pat Obrien's?" Katie asked.

"The one and only," Sinclair said.

"Very cool, Paw-Paw," Katie said.

"Are we taking Phil?" Alana asked.

"If he finishes getting those bags upstairs," Sinclair said. "I think he will need a Hurricane and some fine New Orleans cuisine, don't you?"

"Since Greg won't get in until tomorrow afternoon, we don't have to start work until noon," Nick said, "but we need to start on the case files tomorrow. Sinclair and I will need to have some time late morning to go over some things."

Phil appeared at the doorway of the parlor. "Done," he said.

"Good," Sinclair said. "Now ladies, if you want to retire to your rooms to freshen up, we can leave about seven."

Katie asked, "Now where is the elevator?"

"Go out that door, it leads to the kitchen and go past the pantry, and it will be on your right," Sinclair said.

"Elevator?" Phil asked.

"Yeah," Nick said, "elevator."

"There's an elevator." Phil said.

"Yep," Sinclair said, "goes from the cellar to the attic."

"I could have used an elevator?" Phil said.

"I guess we forgot to tell you," Nick said.

"Well, he didn't ask," Sinclair said.

"No, he didn't," Nick agreed.

"You two are evil old men," Phil said.

Nick and Sinclair laughed.

Chapter 8

After a late night at Pat O'Brien's, one would expect that everyone would sleep in, and they did until seven. They had a great evening with good food, Hurricanes, the dueling pianos, and a flaming fountain. That was last night. This morning it was something different.

A little over a year ago they all worked on solving the crime and bringing the people to justice for the death of Nick Caldwell's daughter and unborn son. Nick had worked the case for years and after he and Sinclair had met, Sinclair and Nick worked the case with help of the others who were part of Caldwell Investigations.

The most binding thing between these two men was that they both knew the pain of what it felt like to lose a child, to have future memories stolen away. They knew each other's pain, never to watch their children grow up; never to see them graduate from high school or college; never to walk their daughters down an isle; never to have grandchildren.

Nick got justice for his child; Sinclair had not.

What they shared was an emptiness. They had moved forward with their lives, but they had never and would never move on until they found those responsible for that emptiness.

Nick had also found out that even if one did find and hold those responsible for the emptiness, it didn't really change that much. Sinclair knew his friend would not find closure because there was no closure for losing a child. You would have to settle for the accountability of finding those who took your hopes and dreams away.

You set out to punish and get revenge, but you eventually settle for what some believe is justice. The joke is there is no justice and no satisfaction in revenge.

Last night, these people celebrated being together to do something important. This morning they rose early to begin the investigation, the journey to get justice for Sinclair's only child.

Nick was sitting in the kitchen with Sinclair, reading the *Times Picayune* over a cup of coffee. As they read Phil and Alana were carting files from Sinclair's office to the elevator and taking them to the ballroom.

Katie and Casey were arranging tables and workspaces so they would be ready when Greg arrived in the afternoon.

"Why don't you and I move into the parlor and go over the basics of the case that you remember," Nick said.

"It's in the file," Sinclair said.

"I know it's in the file, but you and I need to talk about this, the way we talked about the other case," Nick said.

"You're going to make me do this?" Sinclair said.

"I'm not going to make you do anything," Nick said. "I am asking you to help me conduct this investigation."

They walked into the parlor. "What questions do you have?" Sinclair asked.

"I'm not going to ask you questions, I'm asking you to tell me what happened as you remember it," Nick said.

Sinclair sighed. "It was Tuesday night. Tuesday night and Saturday mornings were when dance lessons were scheduled. I was still a detective in the NOLA PD. I was working, so my wife took her to the class. Class started that evening at 6 pm and went to 9:30 pm."

"That was a pretty long class, wasn't it?" Nick asked.

"Sometimes they would go longer if they had a performance coming up," Sinclair said.

"Deidra was in the senior company; she was very talented and dedicated. She had been chosen for a solo in the next recital, and at sixteen that was unusual.

"Margaux was to pick her up after class. She arrived at the studio at 9:15 pm and waited. At 9:30 the other students came out of the building, but Deidra did not. This wasn't unusual because sometimes the principal dancers were a little

28

late coming out after class. Margaux waited until 9:45 pm and went inside to see how much longer she would be.

When she entered, there were no students in the studio.

Barbeau was there and was surprised to see Margaux. She asked where Deidra was and he told her that he was wondering the same thing, that she had not been in class. Margaux told him that she had dropped her off at 5:30. He said that he didn't come down to the studio until right before class and she wasn't there when he took the company attendance.

They looked for her in the building, then Margaux called me. I sent out some officers and went over there. We put out an APB and description and started a canvas of the area. I sent Margaux home and her sister was waiting for her here. She was devastated.

We questioned everyone who was at the studio that night. One of the other dancers remembered seeing her arrive but didn't see her at the class. We questioned the instructors, Barbeau and his son. No one saw her in the building.

Everyone's alibi seemed to check out. Around 2 am my lieutenant told me to go home."

"They continued the search through the night, correct?" Nick asked.

"Yes, I sat up in my office here and listened to the police scanner." Sinclair paused, and Nick could see tears forming in his eyes. Sinclair cleared his throat. "About 5 am, I heard a 187 call from the uniforms, that the body of a young girl had been found in the Quarter by some trash bins. I knew in my heart and my stomach that my baby was gone." Sinclair lit his pipe and looked away. "About an hour later, my captain had them pick me up and take me to the crime scene. I identified her there. She looked so little. The bastard who did this threw her away like a piece of trash."

"Did they have any leads in the beginning?" Nick asked.

Sinclair took a breath. "There was speculation that she may have wandered away from the school into the Quarter.

Maybe she saw someone she knew, maybe someone was lying about their alibi, maybe she was abducted, all the usual theories, but no, we had nothing."

"What was the cause of death," Nick asked.

Sinclair bowed his head and said, "Strangulation." He looked at Nick. "Go ahead ask your question."

"I can get the rest from the autopsy report," Nick said.

Sinclair looked at Nick like he was looking into his soul. "Ask your fucking question."

"Was she assaulted in any other way?" Nick said.

"Ask the question, Nick," Sinclair said.

"Were there signs of any sexual activity or assault?" Nick asked, looking down.

"Yes, there was, the son of bitch raped her before and possibly after he strangled her to death. He basically tore her apart. He strangled her with a pair of tights that he got from her dance pack. Then he stuffed my little girl between two trash bins and piled pallets on top of her. He killed Margaux, too; she never recovered. If anyone asks you if it is possible for someone to die of a broken heart, you tell them it is. I watched my wife die a little each day for three years. She willed herself to death. She never left this house after the funeral. That is why when I find him, I will have a choice to make," Sinclair said.

"I hope one of those choices is bringing him to justice," Nick said, "like you convinced me to do with Mary's killer."

"That is one choice but not the primary choice," Sinclair said, with a faraway cold stare in his eyes, "but not the primary choice I was thinking of. Are we done for now?"

"We're done for now," Nick said.

Chapter 9

The rest of the day was spent organizing the ballroom, going over the case files and waiting for Greg Wells to arrive. Nick met Katie and Greg when he was investigating a case. Greg was a smart kid but with no direction, so Nick introduced him to Felix Coughlan who is a forensic scientist. Greg worked around the office but spent all his spare time before and after work hanging out with Felix. He finished high school and got admitted into Loyola in Chicago and graduated. He joined the agency as Felix's assistant, and he plans to go to graduate school.

Nick was in the ballroom reading the files when his phone rang; it was Greg.

"Hey, Pops, I'm about a half hour away. We had to stop to eat," he said.

"We?" Nick asked.

"Yeah, Sinclair called me yesterday and thought that we would be short handed down there and I was to bring down some extra help," Greg said.

"Who are you bringing?" Nick asked.

"What?" Greg said.

"Who is coming down with you?" Nick said.

"I can't hear you, you're breaking up," Greg said, and the phone went dead.

Nick tried to call him back but there was no answer. He went down to the parlor, where Sinclair was sitting on the couch.

"Did you call Greg and tell him to bring some more folks down?" Nick asked.

"I thought we could use some help, yes," Sinclair said. Bart said he could spare them."

"Do you know who he is bringing down?" Nick asked.

"I told him to bring the best he could find," Sinclair said.

"You didn't ask who?" Nick said.

"Didn't need to, I trust Greg's judgement; you should too," Sinclair said, reading a file.

Nick shook his head and sat down in a chair across from Sinclair. They had been sitting there for about twenty minutes when they heard Greg drive up. Greg knocked on the door and Nick got up to answer it when Sinclair yelled, "Come on in."

The door opened and two streaks ran in followed by Greg. The streaks jumped up on Nick, then immediately, ran to the couch and jumped up and sat next to Sinclair and both received a large dog treat, as Sinclair smiled and received kisses.

"What the hell is this?" Nick asked, looking at Greg.

"Sinclair called and told me to bring Baron and Ruby," Greg said.

Nick turned to Sinclair said, "Why?"

"Greg, tell him what I told you on the phone," Sinclair said.

Greg looked a little nervous.

"Tell him," Sinclair insisted.

"Well, Sinclair said that should bring Baron and Ruby because when they are around, you are not as big of a horse's ass."

Nick looked at Sinclair and said, "Well, it's true."

Phil stuck his head in through the door in the parlor and said, "You need a second for that?"

Baron and Ruby looked at Nick, as if they were in complete agreement.

Nick looked at Greg. "You did bring the equipment we need, right?"

"It's in the van sure; where does it go?" Greg asked.

"It goes to the ballroom on the second floor," Nick said.

Phil said, "Just up to the top of the stairs, a strong healthy lad like yourself ought to be able to manage that easily."

"Okay," Greg said, with very little enthusiasm.

"Greg," Nick said, "there is an elevator in the back of the house."

Greg looked at Phil. "Funny."

"I thought so," Phil said with a grin.

"Just start getting things set up," Nick said.

Sinclair stood up, "There are a couple of dollies back by the elevator, Phil will be happy to get them for you."

"I will?" Phil said.

"You will," Sinclair said.

Baron and Ruby barked their approval and wagged their tails.

Phil looked at them and said, "Traitors."

If dogs could smile, they did.

Chapter 10

By dinner all the equipment, computers, copy machine, eight-foot tables, banker boxes, and a bank of phones had been brought in and set up. The availability of multiple phone lines going into the ballroom puzzled Nick. Maybe a home would have one or two, maybe even three but seventeen?

"Sinclair, I've been wanting to ask you something," Nick asked.

"So, ask," Sinclair said.

"Why are there seventeen phone lines in the ballroom?" Nick said. "That seems like a lot."

"It is," Sinclair said.

Nick looked at him and said, "Well?"

"You know that my daddy was a cop, like your daddy was, and he rose through the ranks to become a chief detective of homicide," Sinclair said, with a little smile.

"I didn't know that," Nick said.

"Yep, the old man lived his life on the straight and narrow; he was a good and honest cop, and in those days it wasn't easy to be that here. Your grandpa was also a cop, right?"

"He was, he was a beat cop and ended up a sergeant," Nick said.

"Well, my grandpa was not a cop; he was a sportsman," Sinclair said, smiling.

"A sportsman?" Nick asked.

"What kind of sportsman? Did he train horses or something like that?" Nick asked.

"He was mostly something like that and then some," Sinclair said.

"What does that mean?" Nick asked.

"Well, Grandpappy established one of the first off-track betting operations in Louisiana, maybe the country," he said, with a hint of pride.

"Your grandfather was a bookie?" Nick said.

"Oh, much more than a bookie. He ran a betting club and provided refreshments. So after the eighteenth amendment was passed, he branched out into imports. He became the roar of the roaring twenties in New Orleans." Nick laughed. "So in 1913, when Southern Bell took over Cumberland Telephone & Telegraph, and consolidation was complete by 1926, he installed those seventeen lines to make it easier to take his patrons' money. From 1916 to until, as my granddaddy would say, 'the business was great until that god damn Yankee from New York,' became president and pushed for repeal in1943, he became a very wealthy man. Business was still pretty good, but he got out of the betting business earlier when my dad decided to join the police force. Didn't want to embarrass him. He went somewhat legit and concentrated on importing whiskey and other spirits. He did pretty well at that too."

"How did your dad take all this?" Nick asked.

"In stride. My granddad asked him one day, right before he became a cop, if he would arrest his own father," Sinclair said.

"My dad said, 'If you are doing anything illegal, I will, Daddy,'" Sinclair said.

"The old man looked at him and said, 'I'm proud of you, son,'" Sinclair said. "The old man shut down all the illegal and questionable aspects of his enterprises and walked the straight and narrow until his death...probably."

"The best thing about the whole thing was there wasn't an establishment that he provided alcohol to in the city during prohibition that didn't at least offer a drink to a Sinclair or a cop who entered the bar until the old man died. And when he died, there wasn't a bartender that didn't wear a black arm ban."

Nick looked at him and they both laughed.

Sinclair said, "Would you like a whiskey before dinner?"

Nick smiled. "I would."

Chapter 11

It was early when Nick rolled out of bed. He showered and dressed and got to the ballroom around 6:30 am. He called Bart in Chicago.

"Good morning, Mr. Cheswick," Nick said.

"I thought I would hear from you yesterday, a young woman called both "Loyola and Michigan to inquire about one Nicholas Spencer Neff," Bart said.

"How did you handle it?" Nick asked.

"We asked for her name, and student number," Bart said. "She declined and we told her that we do not give information about faculty or students to anyone who will not identify themselves or who are not affiliated with the university."

"I'm a little surprised, I thought she might be a little slicker than that, maybe give a phony name," Nick said.

"What time is your meeting," Bart asked.

"Ten," Nick replied, "this is just a scope out meeting."

"Anything else come up?" Bart asked.

"Yeah, Katie and Greg decided to research missing girls who may have met their end the way Sinclair's daughter did over the years from when she died to the present. They want to see if any of them had taken lessons at Barbeau's," Nick said. "Other than that we're just going over files and Greg is going to look at the evidence box and Alana is running down the other dancers who were there that night."

"Wouldn't those folks be in their late forties, maybe early fifties?" Bart said. "They could be hard to track down."

Nick said, "Alana and Phil are going to work on that when Phil gets done putting together the building blueprints. In an old building like this one, we're looking for..."

"For secret rooms?" Bart said.

"Let's say inconsistencies in renovations," Nick said.

"Secret rooms," Bart said.

36

"Based on the police reports, she was raped and strangled, then raped again. The police report stated that a pair of her dance tights were found around her neck, but the autopsy report didn't mention that any fibers from the tights were found on her neck," Nick said.

"You think that she was strangled by hand and the tights were a clumsy attempt to misdirect?" Bart asked.

"Not sure," Nick said. "If it was a clumsy attempt, it worked."

"So, what are you thinking?" Bart asked.

"I'm thinking that she was raped and strangled in one place and the body was removed and dumped in an alley less than a mile from the dance studio. That is why we are looking at the building plans to see if there would have been a way to get the body out of the building and transport it to the alley without being seen."

"Good luck with that," Bart said. "Let me know if you need anything."

"Do you have Cal Simon assigned to anything right now?" Nick asked.

"No, why do you need him down there?" Bart asked.

"I don't know yet, but if I do can you spare him?" Nick asked.

"Sure, he really dislikes the corporate work almost as much as you do," Bart said. "Call if you want me to send him down."

"I will," Nick said. "I'll give you a call after the meeting."

Nick hung up the phone. He began to think that it might be a good idea to have Cal Simon come down. He was a veteran detective from the Chicago PD, and he had spent years undercover. After working on the case that brought Nick's daughter's murderers down, he retired from Chicago PD and joined the new Caldwell-Cheswick Investigations. He didn't have a close relationship with Sinclair. He would be objective, at least more objective than the rest of the crew.

He picked up the phone again and called Bart, "Hey, can you get Cal down here later today?"

"I just told him to pack a bag and get to the airport," Bart said. "Great minds, huh?"

"You got that right," Nick said.

Chapter 12

Nick arrived at the Barbeau Dance Center promptly at ten. The same young woman whom he had made the appointment with was sitting at the reception desk.

"Good morning," Nick said, without his best charming smile. "I am here to see Monsieur Barbeau, my name is Neff."

She looked up and said, "Do you have an appointment?"

Nick replied, "I do, I made it with you two days ago."

"Oh, yes, you're interested in historic buildings," she said.

"Correct," Nick said, "by the way do you need any information on me, I would be happy to show you my faculty IDs."

The young woman blushed. "That won't be necessary, Mr. Neff. Mr. Barbeau is running a little behind schedule, he asked me to ask you if you would like a tour of our facilities until he is free?"

"That would be delightful," Nick said. He did wonder if Monsieur Barbeau had been demoted in the last two days.

A man in excellent shape in his mid-forties appeared at the desk and stuck his hand out. "Mr. Neff, I'm Francois Barbeau, the assistant director here, I would be happy to show you around."

He shook his hand and decided that he would suck his stomach in a little on the tour.

Francois was very proud of what he and his father had built; he was also very proud of his son who had joined his father and grandfather at the dance center.

"This really is a family business," Nick said.

"It is and our family extends to all our students and former students," Francois said.

"Do you keep in contact with your former students," Nick asked.

"We do, they support us in every project we have done," Francois said.

As they toured the basement, Nick said, "I am primarily interested in the structure and the improvements and changes that have been made over the years."

"When my father purchased this building in 1968, it was in terrible condition, It took from '68 to Christmas 1971 to open." Francois said.

"How were you able to finance the renovations on such a large space?" Nick enquired.

"My great grandfather and grandfather did very well and owned several banks in Louisiana. My father worked for them too, but his passion was always dance," he said.

Nick wondered what other passions his father had.

Nick noticed that there were not one but two freight elevators in the basement and asked why would they need two freight elevators?

"We have this basement and a sub-basement we use for storage of scenery, props and costumes that we do not use every season, and we store those we do use in this basement. You will notice that one of the elevators is much nicer than the other. They both go to the top floor, but we use the nicer one and the elevator in the lobby to go into the areas of studios, offices and meeting rooms," he said. "Shall we take one and go to the third floor? You have seen the lobby and the performance space on the first floor. We also have a greenroom and several dressing rooms. On the second floor there is a balcony for the performance space and the offices are up there as well. I am sure when you meet with my father, he will show you all that."

When they arrived on the third floor it was a maze of smaller rooms with dance bars and floor to ceiling mirrors and sound systems in each. It was very impressive.

Francois continued the tour with enthusiasm. "On the fourth floor we have a gym, work out rooms and our training room. There are whirlpools, a sauna and ice tubs. Our training room rivals the Saints or the Pelicans' facilities."

Nick was impressed and wondered if the Bears were blessed with such a facility, but probably not. "What's on the fifth floor?"

"Really nothing, it's just an old open space; we haven't really renovated that space," Francois said.

"I'd love to see it," Nick said.

"I would love to show it to you, but there could be a liability problem with our insurance company," Francois said.

Nick always believed that everyone has something to hide. He smiled and said, "I promise I wouldn't sue you if I fell down." He said it with all the charm he could muster.

"I'm sorry but my father would be very upset, it's not safe. Besides," Francois paused, "I don't want you to think my father is odd, but he believes the fifth floor is haunted."

"Haunted?" Nick said. "That's wonderful."

Francois was taken back a little, "No, seriously, he believes there are spirits; he even tried to have it exorcised a few years ago. I will admit there are a few things that have happened that are strange."

"Are you sure we can't go see it?" Nick asked. I would love to go back to Chicago with a ghost story or two. In fact, my best friend and a colleague of mine is a paranormal psychologist. He works with two others investigating the paranormal all over the world. I bet I could get them to fly down here and check it out. They are not those quacks on TV; they are legitimate scientists."

"I'm sorry, but I don't think my father would allow it," Francois said. His cell phone rang, and he answered it. "Yes, we're on the fourth floor; fine, I will bring him down. My father can see you now."

May I ask you a question?" Nick asked.

"Certainly," Francois said.

"Have you ever seen or heard anything that could be construed as supernatural in the building?" Nick asked."

The elevator door opened. Francois smiled and said, "This way, Mr. Neff."

Chapter 13

Francois did the introductions between the elder Barbeau and Nick. Then he politely excused himself.

"Please sit down, Mr. Neff," Fontane said.

Fontane Barbeau sat on the couch and Nick sat across from him in a plush leather chair.

"Did you enjoy the tour of the building?" Fontane asked.

"I did. This is a beautiful facility," Nick said.

Fontane was pleased with the compliment.

Nick asked, "How long did it take you to renovate it?"

"This is our fiftieth year," Fontane said, "so, we've been renovating for fifty years."

They both laughed.

"We began on the first floor so that we would have a performance area and we could do lessons there. Then we did both basements, then this floor and continued on to floors three and four. We have averaged a floor every ten years in terms of getting it just right." He smiled.

"You are a man of patience," Nick said.

"This is my life. As a young man I had to choose between working in the family business which I had no passion for or following my dream. Thanks to the success of the family business and my father's trust in me, I was fortunate enough to be able to follow my passion," Fontane said.

"It sounds perfect," Nick said.

"Let us say almost perfect," he said.

"Almost?" Nick asked.

"Yes, Mr. Neff, from the time this old warehouse was built in the 1800s it was used primarily for cotton, then sugar cane," Fontane said. "Then it was even used to build boats in the mid-1900s."

"That is fascinating," Nick asked, "what kind of boats?"

"During World War II, New Orleans was the site of the development and construction of Higgins boats," Fontane said.

"General Eisenhower proclaimed these landing crafts were vital to the Allied victory in World War II."

"That's quite a history," Nick said.

"Yes, it is," Fontane said, and then looked down.

"Did I say something wrong?" Nick asked. "You seem a little unhappy."

"No, not unhappy," Fontane said. "It's just that over the years this building has seen a lot of tragedy too.

"Really? What kind of tragedy?" Nick asked.

"Mr. Neff," Fontane began...

"Please call me Nick," he said.

"Thank you, Nick," he continued, "there have been many deaths connected with this building, some through accidents during the building of this warehouse, many deaths of those who worked in this building, and tragedy has even befallen those who have danced in this building. There are times I believe that this building is cursed."

Nick looked surprised, then said, "Francois told me I could not tour the entire building, the fifth floor in particular, because..."

Fontane interrupted, "Because his father is an old man and losing his grip on reality and he believes that the building is cursed?"

"No, that is not how he put it; he said that you may believe it is haunted," Nick said.

"I don't believe it is haunted; it is haunted," Fontane said. My son, Ti, and my grandson, Trip, believe I am a foolish old man who is losing his grip, but I know what I have seen and heard here over the years."

"You have witnessed supernatural events, yourself?" Nick asked.

"I have and I do, but my family says my mind is playing games or it's the building settling. It's not the building settling," Fontane said. "They believe, although they are polite enough not to say it, that I am losing my mind. Do you believe in spirits, Mr. Neff?"

Nick thought back to when he believed he saw his daughter, Mary. "I am open to it," Nick said. "In fact, I was telling your son that my closest friend and a colleague at the university is a paranormal psychologist. He works with two others investigating the paranormal all over the world. He's the real deal; they are scientists in the School of Psychology at Loyola in Chicago. Their investigations are confidential. I have worked with them on investigations of buildings in Chicago and the upper Midwest."

"Do they believe?" Fontane asked.

"They approach it using a scientific method and they keep an open mind," Nick said.

"But do they believe, Nick?" Fontane asked.

"I think they do, but publicly they will tell you that they do believe there are things that are difficult to explain and that is why they need to be looked into," Nick said.

"What do they believe privately?" Fontane asked.

"I can't speak for them, but I believe that they know there is something more and sometimes those worlds overlap," Nick said, "and I know for a fact that they don't disbelieve the possibility. They have to be careful; they are scientists and don't want to be characterized as ghost hunters like those on TV."

"Do you think that they might be interested in seeing this building?" Fontane asked.

"I don't know. They are very busy, but I could ask," Nick said, "if you would like me too."

"Could they investigate it without my family or staff knowing or being involved?" Fontane asked.

"That probably would work well for them; they are not looking for publicity or anything like that," Nick said. "Do you want me to contact them?"

Fontane said, "Please do."

They talked a few more minutes, when there was a knock on the door. "Come in," Fontane answered.

It was the young woman from the lobby. "Sorry to interrupt, but the budget meeting is about to start in the conference room."

"Thank you, Ludmilla," he said. "I'll be right there."

She exited, closing the door behind her.

"Ludmilla?" Nick asked.

"This month--she is trying out stage names; last month it was Cabrilla," Fontane said and then they shook hands. "I hope to hear from you again, soon."

"It would be my pleasure," Nicholas Spencer Neff said.

+

Nick walked to his car and made a call. "Bart, the case has taken a turn; could you and Felix come down for a few days?"

"Define what a few days means," Bart said.

"Friday to maybe Tuesday or Wednesday?" Nick said.

"Let me look at the calendar," Bart said.

Nick said, "I think I have found a way to get Greg and Felix into the Dance Center to look for forensic evidence, but I need you to pull it off."

"Felix looks open and I think I can get open. I will just have Bob and Laura cover things," Bart said.

"That's great," Nick said.

"Why do you need me down there?" Bart asked.

"Fontane Barbeau believes his building is haunted," Nick said.

"Is it," Bart asked.

"How would I know, you're the one who talks with dead people," Nick said.

"They don't talk," Bart said. "Why does he think it's haunted?"

"He said that he has heard and seen things," Nick said.

"Is he nuts?" Bart asked.

"I don't think so; he seems sane, and he says there have been a lot of deaths in the building starting in the 1800s. The building has quite a history. He indicated there have been tragedies in the building since they founded the Center in 1971," Nick said.

"Okay, we'll be down," he said. "Are you free to do a ZOOM meeting tonight?" Bart asked.

"Yes, I'll get Greg to set it up and call you with the details," Nick said.

"Talk to you this evening," Bart said. "This sounds like it will be a weird one."

"Who you gonna call, ghostbusters," Nick sang. "Weird is my middle name," he said, with a laugh.

"No, weird is your full name," Bart said. "Bye."

Chapter 14

All the way back to Sinclair's, Nick was bothered. Usually, he was cynical and suspicious after interviewing a suspect or looking into a case. As a kid, he was suspicious that when he opened a box of Cracker Jack someone might have lifted the prize out of the closed box. He had always had not a sixth sense but a seventh sense; he saw right through guilty people. When he was on the Chicago PD, some of the cops said, Nick had "scumdar," the ability to separate the scumbags from the good citizens with a single look. Nick laughed at this, and would say, if you consider that the vast majority of the people that he was in contact with were scumbags or potential scumbags, it wasn't that hard to pick them out.

The problem today was that he didn't get that kind of vibe from Fontane Barbeau. As he spoke with him no bells or sirens went off. In fact, Nick liked him, and Nick doesn't like many people that aren't in his family or work with him. He didn't know why he liked Barbeau, but he did. There was no sign of deception, no sign of hiding anything. After all he was a complete stranger and Barbeau was open about his belief in the supernatural.

Nick knew that he would have to tread lightly around Sinclair. He was convinced that Barbeau was their guy, but what bothered Nick was that belief was not based on fact and evidence as it usually was with Sinclair; it was based on a feeling he got in a dream. Nick kind of laughed for a minute. Sinclair and Barbeau in some ways were more similar than they were different. At any rate, he was not going to suggest that Sinclair invite Barbeau over for a bar-b-q to trade ghost stories.

+

Nick walked in the door and was greeted by Greg, "Hey, Pops."

"Greg, can you set up a ZOOM meeting..."

"Already scheduled, Bart called a few minutes ago. The invites have been sent," Greg said. His voice got quiet, "Bart told me that you, Casey, Cal and I will be on the call. He thought it would be best if Sinclair was not involved. He told me to have Katie and Alana get him out of the house."

"Good, Cal getting situated all right?" Nick asked. "I didn't see him this morning before I left."

"His plane got in late, and you were already asleep when he got here," Greg said.

"I bet Alana was glad to see him," Nick said. "They are a weird couple, sort of like that character Thomas Shelby from *Peaky Blinders* is dating Tinkerbell and they both have black belts and are qualified in the use of most lethal weapons."

"Yeah, but think about how much fun it will be, if they get married, to watch how they will decide who will carve the turkey at Thanksgiving," Greg said, with a smile.

Nick laughed. "Think about who will get first cut on the wedding cake. Where is everybody?"

"Alana and Katie are with Sinclair trying to convince him to take them on a carriage ride tonight, and Casey, Phil and Cal are in the ballroom, going over files. Hey, do you have a recording for me?"

"Listen to it and see what you think and send it to Felix and Bart to get their opinion of it before we meet tonight," Nick said.

"You were there, did you detect any deception?" Greg asked.

"I want you to listen to it before we talk about it in the meeting. I don't want to influence you. I want everyone to form their own impression," Nick said. "I need to go speak to Sinclair.

+

48

Sinclair was sitting behind his desk being lobbied by Alana and Katie to go out that evening when Nick walked in the room.

"Come on Paw-Paw, we don't know when we will get back here," Katie whined

"Yeah, Alana said, "We want to see the sights."

"Nick may have some work for you two," Sinclair said.

"Nope, if you want to take them out to see New Orleans, they can have the night off. I have to bring Cal up to speed," Nick said.

Sinclair gave Nick the same look his father gave him, when he disapproved of something he did.

"Let me think about it," Sinclair said.

Katie and Alana gave Sinclair the appropriate pouting look.

He looked at them and said, "Okay, maybe."

"That's a start, Paw-Paw," Katie said.

"Ladies, I need the room. Paw-Paw and I have some things to go over," Nick said.

They both stood and walked toward the door; Alana turned and said to Sinclair, "You may call for us at eight this evening, sir."

They left and closed the door behind them.

+

"How did it go?" Sinclair asked.

"It went well, I was given an almost complete tour by the son, Francois," Nick said.

"Almost?" Sinclair asked.

"Yeah, I saw everything but the fifth floor," Nick said.

"Why didn't you see that?" Sinclair asked.

Nick replied, "I was told by the son that it had not been renovated and there were insurance liability concerns."

"Bullshit," was the reply.

"I agree," Nick said.

"You have to get up there," Sinclair said.

"I will, the old man said that he believed it was haunted," Nick said.

"What? Haunted?" Sinclair said.

"Yes, he said that from the time the warehouse was built in the 1800s there had been tragedies and death that were part of the building's history," Nick said.

"That's ridiculous," Sinclair said.

"Maybe, but Fontane believes it," Nick said. "I'm going to have Phil research it."

"We have to get something straight here. I have to run this investigation the way I see fit; it is going to be thorough and systematic," Nick said. "I need your help, but you can't interfere."

"We're talking about my daughter's murder," he said.

Nick looked at him and said, "I am going to do for you what you did for me when we investigated my daughter's murder. I am going to provide objectivity because you can't any more than I could on Mary's case."

Sinclair glared at him, then his look softened. "How are you going to get on that fifth floor; it's likely it could be the…"

Nick interrupted, "the kill room."

"Yes," Sinclair said.

"Barbeau thinks it's haunted. I told him I have friends at the university that are paranormal psychologists who might be willing to come down and investigate," Nick said.

"You're bringing Bart down?" Sinclair asked.

"And Felix and his graduate assistant Greg," Nick said.

"They're going to look for forensic evidence after thirty years?" Sinclair asked.

"If the fifth floor has not been renovated, then it probable has wooden floors. All the other floors in the lobby and hallways, the floors that are not used for dance studios look like the refurbished original floors. The fifth floor has not been renovated; those floors may not be refurbished. We might get lucky."

"What if you don't?" Sinclair said.

"Then we'll lie and get the ghosts to scare the crap out of him until we get him to confess," Nick said, with a half-smile.

Chapter 15

Nick was not a fan of ZOOM calls. In fact, he wasn't a big fan of technology in general, which made him the target of many sarcastic comments about him being a luddite from Phil, Katie and Alana. Greg always thought it was better to not participate in this ribbing of their boss. He recognized its value; he just didn't want anything to do with it.

But here Nick was, sitting looking at a screen that resembled the losers of the auditions for the 60's Hollywood game show. He just wondered which one of them would end up as Paul Lynde or Rosemarie.

"Good evening, everybody," Nick said. "Has everyone been brought up to speed?"

"We have the general idea," Cal said.

"Good," Nick replied, "the plan is simple. Fontane Barbeau believes in the spirit world. The impression I received was that he thinks his building is haunted, but I didn't get the idea that he was concerned that these spirits will harm him. I don't think that he believes that these are the ghosts of the young women who have had an association with the dance studio and the women that have disappeared or met a violent end over the last forty years or so, Deidra being one of them."

"There have been more than Deidra?" Cal asked.

"Yes," Nick replied, "Casey and Katie have been searching for young women over the last four decades that have disappeared or died in questionable ways. They have found seven so far that had a connection with the studio. Six others besides Deidra."

"Were the MOs the same?" Phil asked.

"Not the same, but alike for four of the women; the two others have never been found," Casey said, "and there could be more we don't know about."

"You and Katie stay on this and keep looking," Nick said. "Is there a pattern to the time frame?"

"So far, if they are connected and that's a big if, not really," Katie said, "but we'll keep looking."

"Are you thinking this could be a serial killer?" Cal asked.

"Not yet," Nick said, "but we have to look into it. We have seven young women who are dead or missing and all of them had a connection with the dance academy."

"Are you sure that you can get Felix, Greg and me in there," Bart asked.

"Pretty sure," Nick said. "I think it will be easier if I tell Barbeau you're here and ready to go. When do you think you and Felix can get down here?"

"We can leave tomorrow," Bart said. "I'll call and let you know when tomorrow morning."

"Can we go over what you want us to do?" Felix asked.

"Sure," Nick said. "Barbeau believes his dance center is haunted. The two of you are parapsychologists. You are there to check out alleged psychic phenomena and other paranormal claims, such as apparitional experiences."

"We're quacks," Felix said.

"That's a bit harsh, don't you think?" Nick said.

Phil laughed and said, "Who ya gonna call?"

"Ghostbusters!" Greg said. "Can I be Bill Murray?"

"Seriously, you two have to convince Barbeau that you are on the level." Nick said. "This our chance to get you in a position to do a forensic investigation on the top floor."

"We don't have to wear jumpsuits, do we?" Bart said with a smirk.

"I don't know, Bart. What do you usually wear when you commune with the dead?" Nick asked.

"Depends, will this be formal or casual?" Bart replied.

"You know that finding anything is a long shot," Felix said, "particularly if we are looking for anything that after all these years has the chance of being identified or used in court. That may be virtually impossible."

"We're thinking about this all wrong. We know this is a long shot and we know we probably won't find anything after all these years. Folks, this is a show, we're using this to get in and look around and shake their cages a little bit," Nick said. "The old man believes the place is haunted, so we're bringing our "ghost hunters" in. We know Junior isn't thrilled about this; there is something on that top floor he doesn't want us to see."

"You don't think his son is involved?" Phil asked.

"I'm not saying that, but he may know something, or he is protecting his father," Nick said. "He just seemed very anxious about us going to the top floor."

"What do you want me to do?" Cal asked.

"Katie, Phil and Casey can handle the research, I want you and Alana to start running down the disappearances of the other women. Talk to their families, friends, and other folks who attended the school.

Alana said," Who do we tell them we are?"

"Tell them the truth that you are private investigators that specialize in cold cases," Nick said. "That's what we do, right?"

"And our client's identity?" Alana asked.

"That is confidential," Cal said.

"Or we're independently funded by several foundations," Casey said, "which is true."

"Yeah, The Caldwell and Cheswick Foundation and the Joey "the Bat" Carrandini Foundation," Phil said and laughed.

Hey, the money we get from the Carrandinis is legit," Nick said.

"If it comes from Joey; I'm not so sure about Tony," Phil said.

The Carrandini brothers at one time were part of Chicago's "Outfit," now retired and in legitimate businesses...mostly... hey, it's Chicago.

"It's getting late," Bart said "and Felix and I have to catch a plane in the morning.

"Okay, we'll see you here in the morning," Nick said.

"Whose picking us up?' Bart asked.

"I will," said Cal.

"We should be in by ten," Bart said. "Nick, can we talk for a minute and ask Casey to stay?"

"Sure," Nick said, "hey folks, thanks. Bart and I are going to need the room. Casey, can you stick around too?"

"I can," she said.

They filed out leaving Bart, Casey, and Nick on the ZOOM call.

"What's up?" Nick asked. I hope it is good news."

"It is, sort of," said Bart. "Casey, in the next few days you will receive a call from Arnold Valdez and Mark Silva and Brooke Drake."

"I recognize those names," she said.

"I do too," Nick said, "those are parents of kids that disappeared."

"Correct, but Mark Silva's son, "Wyatt, was't found. I will send you the case file."

"Wasn't he kidnapped and there was a ransom demand?" Nick asked.

"Yes," Bart said, "the Silvas paid the ransom and didn't get Wyatt back."

"That was at least seven years ago," Casey said.

"Right again," said Bart, "all three of these families as you know are wealthy and were burned."

"Why are they calling us," Nick asked.

"They don't want any family to go through what they went through," Bart said.

"And?" Casey said.

"They are setting up a foundation to fund cold cases and cases that the police don't have the resources to handle," Bart said.

"Again, and?" Casey said.

"They want to fund our efforts in cold cases and our investigations," Bart said.

"That's great, but they know what our terms are, correct?" Nick asked.

"I knew you would ask that," Bart said, "and they know."

"They accepted that we have autonomy, and there are no strings attached and they keep out of the investigations?" Nick asked. "They also know that we will not report to them, nor will any member of this team be available to them directly?"

"Yes, they were a little concerned and they wanted to talk to you," Bart said.

"That's not going to happen," Nick said.

"I told them that, too," Bart said.

"Who will be the liaison?" Nick asked. "It can't be Casey because she is staying in the field."

"Casey will be the person that our liaison will contact if we need information," Bart said.

"How much of my time will have to be devoted to this?" Casey asked.

"It won't interfere with your field work," Bart said.

"Are you going to be our liaison?" Casey asked.

"God, no," Bart said, "I think we should have the person who helped put the deal together and handled the initial negotiations with them do it."

"Who would that be?" Nick asked.

"Mrs. Marbles," Bart said.

There was silence on the line.

Then Casey and Nick laughed.

"God help them," Nick said, laughing. "Do they know that if they get out of line, she will shoot them?"

"I think during the negotiations they picked up on the idea that crossing her would not be a smart thing to do," Bart said. "Oh, she also said that she hasn't heard anything from you lately and that you are in trouble, deep trouble, and quote, 'he better get his ass in gear and give me a call tomorrow,' end quote.

"I thought you said this was good news?" Nick said.

"I said good news, sort of," Bart replied.

"I guess I should call her tomorrow morning," Nick said.

Bart laughed. "I think that would be wise."

Chapter 16

Ti stormed into his father's office. "Papa, what do you think you are doing?"

"What's the trouble now?" Fontane replied.

"Is it true that you let that Neff guy talk you into giving your permission for those phony "ghost hunters" to roam all over our building looking for spirits?" his son asked.

"You don't know they are phony, and you must admit that over the years there have been some very strange things that have happened here," Fontane said, "not to mention the other tragedies that are connected to this building. Ti, we have a wonderful studio and we have done beautiful work here over the years, but there is a sense of dread and sometimes it feels like there is an evil presence here."

"Papa, that is utter nonsense," Ti, said. "There is nothing evil here, and there are no spirits here."

"You know that is not true," the old man said.

"I know that old buildings creek and sometimes things do go bump in the night, but spirits? I don't think so," Ti said.

"You are my son and I love you, but I will not be condescended to by you or anyone else," Fontane said. "There are spirits and I have seen them."

"Papa, really..." Ti was interrupted.

"You may leave," Fontane said. "I have things to do before Professor Neth and the others come, and, Ti, you will be cooperative and courteous to our guests; do you understand?"

Ti said, "But Papa, I..."

"Do you understand? Why are you still here?" he said.

Ti left the room angry.

As he walked down the hallway, his son, Trip, was coming toward him. Trip was the third Barbeau, and the family's hope to keep the Barbeau tradition of dance alive through the next century.

He could see his father was angry. "What's wrong, Dad?"

Ti stopped and said, "It's your grandfather; he is on his 'We are haunted, and evil is around every corner' tirade again. I think your grandfather is losing it...again. This time he has invited ghost hunters to prowl around here."

"Cool," Trip said.

"Cool? That is your response?" Ti asked. "It's rubbish and an embarrassment."

"Dad, did you ever think there may be something to it?"

"Trip, there are no spirits, no ghosts, no poltergeists and no aura of evil in this building," Ti said.

"I don't know, Dad," Trip said. "A lot of the people who have worked or rehearsed here late at night have said they had heard things on the top floor and even a few said that they had seen things out of the corner of their eye late at night when the building was quiet."

"Really? Tell ne their names so I can fire them," his father said. "Trip, there are no such things, here or anywhere."

"What will it hurt to have these people come in and take a look?" Trip asked.

"The harm will be to our reputation," Ti said. "What's next, should we solicit ads for our programs from the local Voodoo shops? Should we rent out our theatre space for seances? Should we make every day, the day of the dead at Fontane Barbeau's Ghostly Dance Emporium?"

"I'm only saying that it couldn't hurt," Trip said.

"It could hurt and why are you so interested in this?" Ti asked. "Oh no, don't tell me, really Trip?"

"I'm just saying there have been some strange things happen around here some times," Trip said.

"You have spent way too much time around Papa," Ti said.

"There are hundreds of stories, maybe thousands of stories of ghosts in New Orleans, particularly around the French Quarter," Trip said.

Ti replied, "Keyword here is stories."

Trip looked down and became very quiet.

"What?" Ti asked.

"I have seen one," Trip said, quietly.

"You have seen one? I knew I should have sent you to a public university," Ti said. "Where did you see a spirit?"

"I don't want to talk about it," he said.

"Where!" Ti demanded.

Trip began, "I was walking in the Quarter around last Christmas; I was on my way back here. I was walking behind some of the bars, and I saw a girl, and she was dressed in clothes from the eighties."

"So?, This is new Orleans, the home of weird and everything old is new again," Ti said.

Trip blurted out, "This was different!"

Ti looked at his son. "And how was this different?"

"She looked at me, no she looked through me, she looked as if she recognized me," Trip said.

"That wasn't a ghost; it was probably a French Quarter hooker," Ti said.

"Just stop, Dad, I'm serious," Trip said.

"That is what I am afraid of, son," Ti said.

"Why do think it was a ghost, Trip; had you been drinking?" Ti asked.

"No, she was different, and she had a bag with her," Trip said.

"A bag? What kind of bag?" Ti asked.

"She had a dance bag," Trip said.

"A dance bag?" Ti said.

"Yes, like the old ones we have stored on the top floor," he said, like the ones we used to give members of the company."

"I see. It was a ghost who, what, was a member of our company in the eighties?" Ti asked.

Trip spoke slowly, "I don't know, but she followed me back here and I was scared. When I got back here, I locked the doors and went into the office and..."

"What?" Ti asked.

"When I walked out of the office to check the performance space, she was in our lobby." Trip said.

She walked past you?" Ti said.

"Yes," Trip said, "she walked to the stairway and began to walk up the stairs. I called out and asked where she was going and she turned, she looked scared, and she just pointed."

"She pointed at you?" Ti asked.

"No, Dad, she turned and looked at me and pointed up, I think she was crying and then she was gone."

"Your ghost was crying, pointed up and then she was gone," Ti said, mocking his son. I'm going to tell you this once and only once. Don't ever tell that ridiculous story again, particularly to those idiots your grandfather has invited here. Do you understand?"

Trip looked at his Dad and said, "No, I don't. I don't understand anything about that night."

Chapter 17

Phil met Bart and Felix at the airport and brought them directly to Sinclair's. Katie greeted them at the door.

"Where's Sinclair?" Bart asked.

"Out," Katie said.

"Out?" Felix asked.

"Sinclair agreed that it would be best if he did not directly participate in the investigation," Katie answered.

"How did Nick get him to agree to that?" Bart asked.

"Well, there was a lot of yelling and a lot of cursing and a lot of Nick throwing Sinclair's advice back at him from the Crowe case. Finally, after the yelling stopped, they sat on the couch in Sinclair's office, drank whiskey, and smoked their pipes. The next morning, Sinclair reported to Casey to work on the files," she answered.

"I'm surprised that there wasn't a duel on the riverbank the next morning," Felix said.

"I have come to realize that Nick is a younger version of Sinclair or Sinclair is an older version of Nick. Pops is closer to Sinclair's temperament than he is to Billy's, and he is his dad," Katie said.

"I've known Nick and Billy a long time and Billy is more like the older Caldwell son, Wil, than he is to Nick," Bart said, "and that's understandable. Wil is Chicago PD homicide, like Billy was, gold shield and by the book. Nick is more of whatever it takes. Their relationship has not been the same since he left CPD to do private investigations. Billy's dream was that one day there would be three gold-shield Caldwells in the department."

"He thought Phil would also go into the department?" Katie said.

"Oh yah," Felix said. "He almost had Phil ready to apply, but Phill, right before he was going into the academy, said no. The old man was pissed. He didn't speak to Nick or Phil for a long time, and sometimes it seemed like he was ashamed of Nick, then angry at Nick and Phil for their success as investigators."

"Why's that?" Katie asked.

"He thought Nick's success was detrimental to Wil's career and he was upset that Phil joined what he saw as Nick's side rather than become a CPD officer. You have to remember that all of Billy's family were cops, and most of his wife's family were CPD with the exception of three of her black sheep brothers."

"Black sheep brothers?' Katie asked. "Did they become perps?"

Bart smiled. "No, worse, defense attorneys."

"Billy must have been thrilled when Nick got a law degree," Katie said.

"You're right, it was a dark day for the Caldwell Clan," Bart said. "Where is everyone?"

"In the ballroom waiting for you," Katie said.

"Ballroom?" Felix said.

"Yeah, ballroom," Katie responded, with a laugh.

"Being a detective in New Orleans must pay better than being one in Chicago," Felix said.

"Come on, follow me," Katie said, and they walked up the center staircase to the second floor.

+

They entered the ballroom and Casey greeted them, "Good to see you two."

"A ballroom?" Bart said.

"Who knew that Sinclair was the laird of a New Orleans manor?" Casey laughed.

"Where is he?" Felix asked.

"He is in the second floor library," Casey said.

"Opposed to the …" Bart started to say.

"The first and third floor library or den," she answered.

Bart looked at Felix and said, "Of course."

"Of course," Felix replied.

"The library is at the end of the hallway; he's in there reading some files I gave him earlier," Casey said.

They walked down the hall and came to the door. "Should we knock?"

"It seems appropriate," Bart said and knocked.

"Come in," Nick called.

They walked in and Bart said, "Are you the foreman of this plantation, sir?"

"Not quite, the plantation owner is a little miffed with me," Nick said.

"I heard," Bart said.

"So how are we going to run this charade," Felix said, "and where is Greg?"

"Good to see you, Felix," Nick said, with a laugh.

"I'm not accustomed to being in the field or being part of one of your theatrical productions," Felix said.

"Felix, don't worry, you play a scientist looking for evidence," Nick said, "doing things like you do all the time."

"What's the plan?" Bart asked.

"I have made a few changes, but it is still very simple," Nick said. "You and Felix are the lead scientists. Greg, Katie and Cal will be your associates. We are scheduled to go in tomorrow morning early to meet with Fontane at 7 am.

"I have permission from Fontane for you to be there for several days as long as you don't interfere with their business. Now Ti, the son, will be hostile to you. He thinks the old man is losing it and he will probably try to keep you out of places, like the top floor. We have Fontane's permission to go anywhere we want. Felix, while you are doing the forensics, Bart will be doing the paranormal investigation. Greg will assist Felix and Katie will assist you, Bart. Cal's job is to nose around the staff, and I will be handling the old man.

"Trip is the grandson. This morning we found out apparently, a while ago, he made inquiries at a local voodoo shop about spirits and asked about researching spirits in the French Quarter. He might be a believer, maybe he has experienced something, or maybe he is just supportive of his grandfather. Bart, you need to get close to the kid."

"Do you think he may have experienced something or is he just reacting to something he has seen or heard?" Bart said.

"Don't know. Maybe have Katie do the first contact with him, he's a healthy young man, he might want someone less threatening to confide in," Nick said.

"He doesn't know Katie," Bart said, with a smile. "May I ask you a question?"

"What?" Nick answered.

"Do you think Fontane had anything to do with the murders?" Bart asked.

"I don't know," Nick said, "maybe or maybe he's covering something up, maybe he suspects something."

"What about the son?" Felix asked.

"He seems to be protective of his father, but he is a little too intense." Nick said. "We're going to have to give him a good look. Cal is following that up. He is not a likable guy, but he tries to look like he is."

"Nick, what's our end game?" Bart asked.

"What it always is, find the bad guy or guys and make them accountable," Nick said.

"To whom?" Bart asked.

Nick smiled. "To whomever they need to be accountable: the justice system, the families, to Sinclair."

Chapter 18

The next morning the crew arrived at the dance studio, Dr. Nicholas Neth, Dr. Jonathon Bartholomew, Dr. Conrad Flexman, Dr. Alphonse Calvin, Mr. Bradley Gregory and Ms. Katherine Neth, daughter of Professor Neth and a graduate student in the study of the paranormal.

The same young woman that Nick encountered in his previous visits was at her post, doing what she did best: securing the gate, ensuring that no one gets past her unless they were supposed to be there. This morning her instructions were clear; they will not see Fontane until they have a talk with Ti in the conference room.

"I'm sorry Professor," she said, as if she knew this was a con, "but before you can see Mr. Barbeau Sr., Ti would like to speak to you and your entourage in the conference room."

Usually Nick would have walked past her and said something that would be insulting at best, but he wasn't Nick, he was Professor Nicholas Neff. "It would be my pleasure to speak with Ti again." And being charming, he continued in the same tone she had used to address him, "Ti is almost as delightful as speaking with you," he said with his best insincere smile.

She raised her eyebrow and said, "Why thank you, mister, I mean professor."

Nick was beginning to warm to this twenty something smart ass. He smiled again and said, "Lead on."

They followed her to the elevator for the short ride to the second floor. When they arrived at the conference room they found Ti sitting at the end of the table.

"Ti, it's so good to see you again," Nick said ,extending his hand.

Ti did not take it; instead he said, "What are you really doing here?"

Nick looked confused. "I don't understand. Your father requested that we investigate the paranormal activity in your building."

"My father is a superstitious and delusional old fool," Ti said.

"He didn't impress me that way," Nick said. "He was rational in our conversations."

"You're wrong, and I don't want you here," Ti said.

"Your father does, so that is why he had me bring these people down here," Nick said.

"What's the game here? How much is he giving you for 'your investigation.' I want to know," he said.

"Giving us?" Nick asked.

"Let me put it another way, how much do you plan to extort from a crazy old man who needs help?" Ti demanded.

"Oh, 1.2 million dollars," Nick said.

"What?" Ti said, in disbelief.

Nick laughed at him. "Are you sure it's your father that needs help?"

"I know that this is a scam, and you are trying to take advantage of a senseless old fool," Ti yelled.

From behind them they heard, "He is not old fool."

Standing in the doorway was Trip.

"This is none of your concern," his father said. "Leave now."

"I don't think that will be necessary," came from behind Trip; it was Fontane Barbeau. "This senseless old fool says that Trip stays. In fact, Professor Neth and his associates will stay as well, and you will go back to your office, and we will discuss this later."

"I'm only trying to protect you and our business," Ti said.

"We will discuss it later," Fontane said sternly. "Leave us, now!"

Ti looked like he had something else to say but thought better of it and stomped out, glaring at his father, his son and Nick.

"Please, Professor, won't you and your colleagues please sit down, and we can discuss your investigation," Fontane said. "But first I want to apologize for my son's behavior. He has always had a terrible temper; when he doesn't get his way or what he wants his anger is explosive. I also want to introduce my grandson, Trip. He is just the opposite of his father in many ways. He will also be finishing up his business degree at Loyola here in New Orleans, and I hope one day he will manage our business."

"Mr. Barbeau, there is no apology needed, and it is our pleasure to meet you, Trip," Nick said. "We are happy to have the opportunity to do the investigation."

"May I ask you a question, Professor?" Fontane asked.

"Certainly," Nick replied.

"How do you want the 1.2 million paid in?"

Nick was taken aback, then he saw the glint in the old man's eyes. "A check or cash would be fine." Both men erupted into laughter.

"Seriously, Professor, may I help with your expenses?"

"Thank you for the offer and it is appreciated, but we are funded for projects like this by our organizations, the university and a private foundation," Nick said, and he could almost read what Bart was thinking: "If only that were true."

If I cannot pay you the 1.2 million, then may I offer you and your associates coffee and lunch while we discuss the project?" Fontane said.

"That would be nice," Nick said.

"Good, I have asked Trip to stay with us and be my liaison between you and your team." Fontane said.

"That's fine, but Dr. Bartholomew and Dr. Flexman are our team leaders," Nick said.

"Dr. Bartholomew, Dr. Flexman, it is good to meet you," Fontane said.

"It is an honor to meet you Mr. Barbeau," Bart said.

"I don't want to meddle in your investigation, but may I suggest, after lunch you begin by speaking to my grandson, he has had a very interesting experience that I believe may be of interest to you and the investigation," Fontane said.

"We would be happy to," Bart said.

Nick looked at Bart and they were thinking the same thing: Trip had a reason for the visits to the voodoo shops in the Quarter.

Chapter 19

After lunch, the "paranormal team," Trip and his grandfather sat around the conference table.

"Go on, Trip, tell them what you saw," his grandfather said.

Trip began the story that he had told his father, the story that his father said that he should never repeat. When he had completed his story, the "team" had some questions.

Nick asked, "Did you recognize this woman?"

"No, I had never seen her before," Trip answered.

"Trip, maybe you never saw her in person but maybe you've seen a picture of her," Bart said.

"I don't know," Trip said.

"You said that she carried an old dance bag from the studio," Bart said. "Do you have an archive of photographs that we could look at?"

"We do," Fontane said. "I'm sure that our Grace, our communications director, could help."

"Could Dr. Calvin meet with Grace?" Nick asked.

"I will arrange it as soon as we're done here," Fontane said.

"Fontane, you mentioned that a significant amount of tragedy is associated with this building," Nick said.

"That is true," Fontane replied.

"Has any of that tragedy been during the time that you have owned the building?" Bart asked.

"Yes, when we were doing the rehab in the beginning a workman died in an accident," Fontane said.

"Anything else," Nick asked.

"What do you mean," Fontane asked.

"Well, has there been anyone connected with the studio or worked at the studio that have had tragic episodes or ends? Nick asked.

"Not on the premises," Fontane said.

"Have there been people connected with the studio who met with tragedy off the premises?" Bart asked.

"I am afraid so," Fontane said. "We have had several who have been part of the company over the years that have been victims of violence in the surrounding neighborhood, nothing connected to the studio. They were more like wrong place, wrong time. These kinds of things can happen from time to time in the Quarter if one is not careful and..."

Nick asked, "What is it, Fontane?"

Fontane, cleared his throat, "There have been a few of our dancers over the years that just disappeared."

"Disappeared?" Bart asked.

"Yes, a few of our dancers that were part of the company just left without a word and we never heard from them again," Fontane said. We eventually were contacted by the police, and we found they had disappeared from their families and New Orleans. No one has heard from them again."

Considering Trip's experience, it might be helpful if we knew the names and had information on everyone who may have disappeared or met a tragic end," Bart said. "Is there anyone that could help us with that? If we are going to investigate any spiritual activity, it would be a help."

"Yes, I'm sure my son would have or know where we have that information," Fontane said.

"Kathrine, could you follow up with, Ti is it?" Bart said.

"Yes," Fontane said.

"I will speak to him this afternoon," Katherine said.

"Fontane, will Dr. Bartholomew and Dr. Flexman have access to the building? I remember Ti had some hesitation allowing me to see the fifth floor," Nick said.

"Ti is very protective of the studio," Fontane said. "He rejects the idea that there could be something beyond our understanding going on here, or for that matter, anywhere else in the world. But I will instruct him that you will have full access to the building."

"Thank you," Nick said.

"Would it be too much of an imposition if I asked you to be discreet," Fontane asked.

"Not at all. What do you have in mind?" Nick asked.

"Ti does have a point about bad publicity," Fontane said. " I was wondering, since we don't have performances in the building this month and our classes end around 8 pm and we end rehearsals at 10 pm would it be possible if your search for paranormal activity could begin after 10 pm, after the building is empty?"

"That is fine with us," Nick said. "Is that okay with you Jonathon?"

"Perfect, I understand that our presence could raise questions from your staff and students. There are things that are less intrusive we can do during the day, for example, researching the building's history looking at your archives. If anyone asks, we will tell them that Nicholas is working on an historical project about historical buildings," Bart said.

"That's perfect," Nick said, "since I am working on a project of historical buildings."

"Thank you," Fontane said. When would you like to begin?

"Well, if Dr. Calvin could meet with Grace this afternoon and Conrad and I could take a look at the fifth floor this afternoon, we could start this evening," Bart said.

"Excellent," Fontane said.

"May I ask you a question?" Nick said.

"Certainly," Fontane said.

"You mentioned that there were a few young women associated with the company that disappeared or had a tragic end," Nick said.

"Sadly, that is true?" Fontane said.

"Do you remember any of their names?" Nick asked.

Fontane looked down. "I remember all of their names," his voice trailed off.

"Is there any one of them that you remember more than the others?" Nick asked.

Fontane looked as if he were on the verge of tears. "Yes."

"Who would that be?" Nick asked.

"She was a beautiful and lovely young woman, Fontane began. "She started taking dance lessons very young, she had a gift. She was bright and intuitive. She came from an old New Orleans family. She understood dance.

"Her mother was a professional dance before she married. She was a wonderful and kind person. I had known her grandfather. He was an eccentric man. He was one of our first benefactors. I got to know her father well too. He became a benefactor after his father passed on. In fact, he and I became friends. I will never forget their tragedy. After their daughter was killed and the murderer wasn't found, her mother died of a broken heart. They say that can't really happen, but I believe it did in this case. That girl meant everything to her mother and father. It destroyed her father as well. He was rising rapidly in his career, after he lost both his wife and daughter, he began to drink. He was full of rage and finally, he just quit his job and left New Orleans."

"What happened to him?" Nick asked.

"He came back after about a year and started a small business, but most of his time was spent searching for his daughter's killer. He was obsessed," Fontane said.

Nick looked at Bar, then asked Fontane, "Where is he now?"

"He's in New Orleans, lives in his family's home, still has his business, but the last few years he has worked up north a lot," Fontane said. "I miss him. We used to have lunch together at least three times a month. He had fascinating stories."

"Sounds like you liked the guy," Nick said.

"I did, but after his daughter died, he changed. I think he blamed me for what happened," Fontane said.

"Blamed you, why?" Bart asked.

"Her father said that we were located in a high crime area and that we needed to take better precautions with

73

security around the building," Fontane said. "We were contracted with a security company, but they were there to secure our building and she was murdered blocks away."

"That's a terrible story," Nick said.

"It had an impact on my family too," Fontane said.

"On your family?" Bart asked.

"Yes, Ti was a few years older than Deidra and had a crush on her. After she was killed he was never the same," Fontane said. "Well, I should take Dr. Calvin to meet Grace and your daughter to Ti's office, so you can get started.

'The girl's name was Deidra?" Nick asked.

"Yes, Deidra Stewart," Fontane said.

Chapter 20

After Fontane left the room, Nick turned to the team and said, "Bart and I are going back to Sinclair's. Felix, see if you can get on the fifth floor and start looking around."

"This isn't good," Felix said. "What else didn't he tell us?"

"Good question," Nick said.

"How are you going to handle it with him," Bart asked.

"I don't know. This could mean that the information he got about Fontane isn't information but a way to get revenge," Nick said. "Can't find the real murderer, somebody has to pay. Why not make the guy who didn't secure his building the way you told him to, pay."

"You don't really think that's what he is doing, do you?" Bart asked.

"I don't know. Maybe the most rational guy I have known can't be rational about this," Nick said.

"Come on, Nick," Bart said. "You were ready to go all O.K. Corral over the Crowes after you found out that they were responsible for your daughter's death."

"I was," Nick said, "but I didn't, did I. I didn't withhold any pertinent information from you or anyone else we were working with."

"You know, if you go in there as pissed off as you are now, you won't get anything from him, right?" Bart said.

"Yeah, that's why you're going with me, "Nick said.

"You know Fontane's story could be bullshit," Bart said. "They also may have figured out we're not who we say we are. We don't know these people. Do you believe him?"

"I don't know what to believe," Nick said. "That whole thing about Ti having the hots for Deidra and being changed forever was strange. He's pretty pissed off at Ti. Do you think he could be getting ready to throw him under the bus? Let's go talk to Sinclair."

Bart and Nick got back to Sinclair's and were met by Casey. "What the hell is going on? Katie texted and said that Sinclair knew this guy well?"

Nick looked at her and said as calmly as he could, "Where is he?"

"In his library," she said.

Bart and Nick walked to the door of the library and knocked.

"Come in," Sinclair said.

Bart and Nick entered the room and sat across the desk from Sinclair.

He looked at them and said, "What's up?"

"We need to talk, now," Nick said.

"Okay," Sinclair said, "shoot."

Nick looked at him and said, "I'd like to."

Sinclair looked at him. "What's up your butt?"

"Let me ask you a question, when are you going to start leveling with us and quit withholding pertinent information?" Nick said. "Because if you are not going to do that then I'm going to ask Bart to pack up the circus and go back to Chicago."

"I don't know what you are talking about?" Sinclair said.

"You and Fontane Barbeau were friends," Nick said.

"We knew each other a long time ago," dismissed Sinclair.

"You had lunch with him almost every week," Bart said.

"So?" Sinclair said.

"So people who meet almost every week and there is no business consideration are probably friends, and people who are friends don't usually point the finger at a friend without more proof than 'I just know.' For God's sake, Sinclair," Nick said, "what the hell is going on here?"

"It's not important to the case," Sinclair said.

"Not important that you have had a friendship with the person you have identified as the person who killed your daughter?" Nick asked. "That's crazy."

"It was a long time ago," Sinclair growled.

"Your daughter's murder was a long time ago," Bart said.

"Here is where we are, either you play straight with us or we are out of here," Nick said.

"Are you giving me an ultimatum?" Sinclair said.

"No, my friend, it is a statement of fact," Nick said. "There are nine people and two dogs that are down here because they care about you and admire you and they want to solve this case, knowing there is no closure for you, but they want you to at least have justice and know what happened. Every one of them is working with just expenses being paid by that man over there who is kind enough to indulge me when I take off on one of these cases and we care enough for you that we have most of our best people down here for you.

"Mrs. Marbles, Laura and Bob, my sister and brother in-law and Constance have asked if they come down on their own dime to help. Dad and Dalton contacted Bart to see if there was anything they can do. Even my brother Wil asked if he could help and our Italian friends, Joey and Antonio wanted to help.

"That's exactly what we need, a CPD Chief of Detectives, two broken down old cops and two Chicago wise guys to come down here," Sinclair said.

"You know, I have always said, this is a business, we catch bad guys, period. Bart always corrects me and says we are a family business that catches bad guys. He's right."

Bart said, trying to cut the tension, "Could you say that again so I can record it?"

Sinclair almost smiled, "What about your Missy?"

"My Missy? No, I have not heard from Maureen in a while," Nick said, "and she is not my Missy. The woman is trouble and possibly lethal. Maureen, well she is Maureen, and

I would never be sure of her getting over me shooting her sister."

"That's pretty narrow minded of her since her sister was planning on killing you and another hostage," Bart said.

"Can we stop reminiscing about the good old days and her devotion to killing me and get back to what we are doing here?" Nick said.

"Sinclair, if we are going to continue, we really need you to tell us everything," Bart said. "Why don't you take a little time to think it over and decide what you want to do and what you want us to do."

"Did that work when you were a shrink," Sinclair asked.

"I wasn't a shrink, I was a counselor" Bart said, "and yes, it did work."

"How well," Sinclair asked.

Bart smiled. "To the tune of two hundred- fifty dollars an hour towards the end. Just think about it. We can talk about this later tonight; I have to get back to the studio."

Sinclair sat at his desk, clearly not happy, "Fine we can talk later."

"Was that so hard?" Nick said.

Sinclair looked at Bart and said, "Now, get out of here. And take him with you before I shoot him."

"If Maureen couldn't kill me, I don't think you can, old fella," Nick said, with a smile.

"I didn't say I was going to kill you, just shoot you, and remember that she was able to do that," the old fella said. "Now git."

Chapter 21

As Nick pulled into the studio parking lot, Bart asked, "What do you think?"

"With Sinclair? I don't know. We'll see tonight, I guess," Nick said.

"I got a text from Felix; he was able to get up on the fifth floor," Bart said.

"Did he find anything interesting?" Nick asked.

Bart said, "We knew finding any DNA or other forensic evidence was a long shot, but he did find some things he would like to look at closer, but I wouldn't get our hopes up."

"Did he find anything that we could bluff with, if we had to?" Nick said.

"It depends, doesn't sound like there is much there, but maybe we will get lucky at some point," Bart said. "Oh last night I thought I saw someone outside Phil's room. He was making a little noise, so I went back in my room to get my robe and went back out in the hall, and he was gone."

"You probably saw Sinclair's great-great-great uncle, Brigadier General Jack MacGregor Stewart. He died in that room in 1863 from self-inflicted wounds accidently. He was drunk, and I think fell on his sword. He has taken a liking to Phil," Nick said.

"Go figure," Bart said, and they both laughed.

They were greeted by a very unhappy Ti. "You promised that you would not disrupt our business."

"How has your business been disrupted," Nick asked.

"I was treated without any respect at all by that young woman, Katherine," Ti fumed.

Nick replied, "She gets that from her mom, Well, I apologize, but she always has been a good judge of character or lack of it."

"Not funny," Ti said

Nick looked at Bart. "I thought it was funny, didn't you?"

"Well, it was between funny and humorous," Bart replied. "The delivery was good not great."

"Okay," Nick said.

"I am warning you, Neth," Ti said.

"Now he's warning me..., Nick said, "go on."

"Keep that girl away or there will be grave consequences," Ti said through gritted teeth.

Looking at Bart and smiling Nick responded, "Hmm, not just consequences but grave consequences. Did *A Few Good Men* happen to be on TV last night?"

"What?" Ti said, confused. "Just keep that little tramp out of my office."

"You are calling my daughter that? She has had a very difficult life. Her mother divorced me after I shot her sister, self-defense. Things are weird with family at the holidays, aren't they. But it was hard on her; she started learning to shoot and took martial arts classes. She's an expert at weaponry and you called my baby girl a tramp. I am very disappointed in you, Ti," Nick said. "Ti, could you excuse me for one moment?"

Nick walked over to the main desk and asked to use the house phone. He dialed an extension and turned his back to Ti. Excuse me for interrupting you, but I have a difficulty here in the lobby with Ti. In a quiet voice Nick explained the situation and asked if he had permission to solve the difficulty. The voice on the other end listened to how he thought the problem could be solved and gave him the go ahead. He asked to talk to the young woman at the desk. She smiled.

He crossed over to Ti and said, "I think that both my daughter and I deserve an apology."

"That will never happen," Ti said.

Nick looked at Ti and was impressed at what good shape he was in. "Well, I would like it anyway or there will be grave consequences, so please apologize. It's the right thing to do."

Nick looked up at the railing on the second floor where Fontane and trip were watching. Fontane nodded.

"I am going to ask politely one more time," Nick said.

"I am tired of listening to your crap," Ti said, and he took a step toward Nick.

Nick hit him squarely on the jaw and he dropped like a bag of manure, which he was.

Ti shook his head and mumbled, "You assaulted me."

"No, I did a sorely needed attitude adjustment under the supervision of a trained psychologist," Nick said, and Bart took a slight bow.

Ti turned to the girl at the desk. "You saw it," he screamed.

"I'm sorry, I guess I missed it," she said.

Then he looked up and saw his father and son, "Did you see, he assaulted me?"

"Sorry, son, Trip and I were talking," Fontane said.

"May I give you a hand getting up?" Nick asked.

"Get the fuck away from me," Ti said.

"Well, we have a meeting on the fifth floor, so we have to go," Nick said. "Nice seeing you again."

Nick and Bart walked toward the elevator.

"Damn, have you been working out?" Bart asked.

"Nope," Nick said and opened his hand. In the palm of his hand he had a roll of quarters. In the worst Sean Connery imitation ever, he said, "The Chicago way... Nick, Nick Neff."

Bart looked at him, shook his head and laughed.

Chapter 22

In the elevator Bart said, "You know I was really happy to see you unleash your inner Phil."

Phil Caldwell, Nick's youngest brother and a detective with the firm, is best known for his interrogation technique of convincing the subject that he is a psycho, who has scored in the same range as Gacy, Bundy and Ramírez on psych tests. He is quite good and at worst he makes his subjects very uncomfortable, and at best the need to change their underwear.

"Why thank you," Nick said, "I appreciate that. You don't think it was a little over the top?"

"Over the top? No. That story about shooting your wife's sister was very believable and a nice touch," Bart said. "However, you might want to work on the Connery imitation. I think the old Bond line would be better if instead of 'Nick...Nick Neff,' you said 'Neff...Nick Neff.' It's more like the movie, you know Bond...James Bond, it just flows better."

"Well, you may have a point," Nick said. He sat at the conference table and said, "What have we learned today?"

Katie said, "We learned Ti is a jerk and if you punch in the jaw in the absolutely correct place with a roll of quarters in your palm, he actually bounces."

"Did we learn anything that might help us with the case," Nick asked.

"I already told you, Ti is a jerk and we're not going to get anything out of him about the five girls we know about or any new ones," Katie said. "We're going to have to get information from someplace else. I contacted Casey, and she said she would have something for me tomorrow."

"Okay," Nick said. "Did you find anything, Felix, on the fifth floor?"

"Yes and no," he said. "It is used for storage of things they will never use again. I did find something that looked like a blood stain, but it is probably badly degraded. I already overnighted it to the Chicago lab. I should get news back tomorrow or the day after that. Also, I found under some old curtains a couple of mattresses. They were in fairly good shape for their age."

"See if Greg can find anything on them, hair, blood, whatever," Nick said.

"Okay, does anybody know what time it is?" Nick asked.

Katie and Greg responded with *"Does anybody care about time?"* from a Chicago song, from an album that Nick sings from in his office.

"Funny, now go to your room without dinner," Nick said.

Katie gave him her best pouty look with her lip stuck out and everything and said, "About six o'clock."

Nick said, "Why don't you all head back to Sinclair's and get some rest. Bart and I are going to stay here for a while."

"Nick, I would like to stay too," Cal said.

"Fine, if you want," Nick said.

+

By ten-thirty everyone that was still alive had left the studio, with the exception of Nick, Bart, Felix, Greg and Cal. As for the ghosts in the building that would be determined later.

They were all sitting on the fifth floor. Felix and Greg were trying to collect forensic evidence.

"Nick, what we have collected is badly degraded. I have made arrangements with an old friend who's at LSU to use his lab tomorrow, so I think that Greg and I are going back to Sinclair's so we can get an early start for Baton Rouge," Felix said.

"Okay," Nick said.

"Besides, I think the *'ghosties'* might come out if the non-believers head out," Felix said, with a rare smile.

"Oh, ye of little faith," Bart said.

"You know, Bart, I have heard that…" Cal began.

"That I talk to dead people? Commune with the spirits? Get messages from beyond? That sort of thing?" Bart asked.

"In a word," Cal said, "yes, and you don't seem the…"

"The type," Bart replied.

"Are you telling me that you have never heard of Bart Cheswick, the Supernatural Sixth Sense Detective?" Nick said.

Bart laughed.

"Haley Joel Osment is Bart's love child, but we don't like to talk about it because of the back child support payments," Nick said.

"And it would upset my husband," Bart said.

"That too," Nick said.

"How do you go about contacting these spirits?" Cal asked.

"I'm here, if there are spirits, they know or sense that I can communicate with them," Bart said. "Did you ever see that old television show, *Ghost Whisperer*?"

"Yeah," Cal said.

"The lead character didn't really have a choice; they found her and that's kind of the way it is," Bart said.

"Do you think we'll be able to see them?" Cal asked.

"I don't know," Bart said, "maybe if you're open to it."

"Do you talk to them, and do they talk back?" Cal asked.

"I talk to them, but they don't really talk. I kind of pick up what they are feeling and it's more like I can hear them in my head," Bart said.

"Do you remember the McCarty case, the guy wrongly accused and executed, that we worked on a few years ago?" Bart asked.

"Yeah, I read both the books about it," Cal said.

Nick rolled his eyes. "That was fiction."

"Are you ever going to give that guy a break?" Bart asked. "He was very close to what actually happened. Anyway, we went to the town he grew up in and I visited his grave and spoke to him, and there he was."

"Did he help you break the case?" Cal asked.

"He gave us insight," Bart said. "I got a sense of what direction we should think about, and it helped, but Nick broke the case the old-fashioned way, running down leads, intuition and a little common sense."

"I would say more like uncommon sense," Nick commented. "We used Occam's Razor, 'the simplest solution is almost always the best.' In that case, the simplest solution was that his wife wasn't dead and had framed him."

Bart got a strange look on his face, "They're here."

Chapter 23

As Felix and Greg pulled up into Sinclair's drive, they saw the lights on in his study. When they walked in, they found him and heard him asleep in a chair and he was having what seemed to be a very bad dream. They didn't know if they should wake him.

Casey and Katie came out of the kitchen.

"Where's Nick and Bart?"

"They are with Cal looking for ghosts," Felix said. "What's going on with Sinclair?"

"He's having a very bad dream, almost bordering on night terrors," Katie said.

"Should we wake him and get him up to bed," Greg asked.

"I wouldn't," Katie said. "The man sleeps with a revolver on the table next to him; let sleeping Scottish lairds sleep."

"He's been having these dreams a lot since we got here," Casey said. "Best we leave him alone."

"Are you sure?" Greg asked.

"Well, I'm going to bed," Felix said. "I'm sure reliving all this over again has him in a very sensitive emotional state."

"Does Nick know about this?" Greg asked.

"He knows," Phil said, walking down the stairs. "Let the man have his privacy. I'll talk to Nick and Bart in the morning."

"He's going to wake up in a couple of hours, anyway," Casey said. "Then he walks around the house most of the night."

"He may be sleepwalking," Katie said.

"Why do you say that?" Greg asked.

"Because you will sometimes hear him talking," Phil said.

"What's does he say?" Felix asked.

"I've heard him say, 'Is she all right?' Then you hear him walk."

"I heard him ask, 'General, is she here?' Then he will sit for a few minutes, then he is walking again," Phil said.

"Who's the General?" Felix asked.

"His great, great Grandfather who fought in the Civil War," Phil said.

Felix looked at them. "Okay, now I am going to bed."

"We probably all should," Casey said. "Phil, you're going to talk to Nick in the morning?"

"I will," he answered.

They all headed up to their rooms. They heard from office, Sinclair ask, "Deidra, is that you, sweetheart?" Then he mumbled something else.

They all continued to their rooms. There were tears in several of their eyes.

Chapter 24

Cal looked at Nick. "What does he mean?"

"Shhh," Nick hushed him, "he means we're not alone."

You could hear Cal gulp.

"Hello, we mean you no harm. My name is Bart. Could you let me know who you are?"

There was a rush low vibrating sound, and slowly before them a form of a young man appeared.

"You are Peter Dawson?" Bart asked. "Peter what are you doing here? You are a worker at the warehouse? What year is it, Peter? 1904. I don't want to upset you but why haven't you moved on?" There was a pause as Bart listened. "I see."

"What did he say," asked Nick.

"He says he was killed while working on the support beams, he fell to his death," Bart said. "I'm sorry, Peter." Bart looked at Nick. "He wants to know who we are."

"Tell him," Nick said.

"We are detectives, from Chicago," Bart said, and then he smiled. "Sort of but we are not Pinkerton's, why do you ask?" Bart said. "Really? Nick, he says that your manner reminds him of one of the Pinkerton boys."

Nick said, "I'm flattered but no relation that I know of...I guess all Scots look alike."

Bart said, "You made him laugh."

Nick looked at Cal who stood there in half amazement and shock.

"Cal, are you okay?" Nick asked.

Cal nodded and said, "Yes."

"Peter, are there others here?" Bart asked. "There are...do you think they might speak to us?"

"What did he say?" Nick asked.

"He doesn't know. He has been here a while, but because of what has happened in this room they are frightened," Bart said.

"What happened here?" Nick asked.

"He says terrible things happened here. Peter, don't go. Peter, we need your help," Bart said.

The image slowly faded away, and they were alone.

Cal stood silent, then spoke, "Was that real?"

"Did you see him?" Nick asked.

"I did," Cal replied.

"Well, this was either real or we suffered group hysteria. I'm leaning towards real," Bart said.

"What do we do now?" Cal asked.

The first thing tomorrow, we have Phil and Casey research census record, birth records, construction work done to this building around 1904. We'll see if we can turn up a Peter Dawson anywhere," Nick said. "Bart, may I try something before we go?"

"The floor is yours," Bart said.

"My name is Nick Caldwell; in my youth I was a Chicago police detective. I lost my daughter when some bad men killed her. I am here because a close friend lost his daughter. We believe she was taken from him by a bad man. We came to find that bad man. We are here because this man who lost his daughter means a lot to us, and he is suffering. Peter said that he was not alone. I am asking if there is anyone here that has heard or knew a New Orleans' police detective named Sinclair Stewart?"

It seemed his words hung in the air for a moment and the room was silent.

"Well, it was worth a try," Nick said.

"Let's pack up and head back to Sinclair's," Bart said.

They packed up and walked toward the door at the end of the large room. They all were carrying large bags of equipment. They were five feet from the closed door when it opened, as if someone or something was opening it to help them. They looked at each and walked out of the room.

As Nick walked through the door, he said, "Thank you." As they walked down the steps, the door slowly closed.

+

They dove back to Sinclair's. Nothing was said in the car.

When they arrived back, Cal asked, "What are we going to do now?"

"Well," Nick said, "we're going to meet in the morning and the three of us will talk about this and listen to the recording. Then we will get Phil and Casey the information to research. Now we are going to go to bed and get some sleep and if we can't sleep, we will meet in Sinclair's office and drink until we can sleep."

"Sounds like a plan to me," Bart said.

They walked in the door and stored the equipment. Cal went upstairs to his room. Bart and Nick stood in the hallway on the second floor and looked at each other.

"Are you a believer now," Bart asked.

"I will be tomorrow, after I have Felix and Greg go over that room to make sure we weren't at a theatrical séance," Nick said. "Did you leave the micro cameras recording?"

"I did, if anyone goes into that room tonight or early in the morning we'll know," Bart said.

"Trust but verify," Nick said.

"I think that..." Bart was interrupted.

"Me too," Nick said, and began to walk downstairs.

"Hey, aren't you going to try to get some sleep?" Bart asked.

"Yeah, I'm just skipping the first step, then trying to get some sleep for the next step," Nick said, as he headed to Sinclair's office.

Bart watched him go, then said, "Hey, wait up," and followed him down the steps.

Chapter 25

There was a knock at Nick's door early that morning. He was grateful that his head felt like it did, not feeling like a dump truck fell on it. It did feel like a Missouri Mule kicked him several times in the head.

"Come in, if you have to." Phil walked in and sat on the bed across from Nick who had only made it to the chair in his room on the way back from the bathroom.

He looked at his younger brother and said, "What the hell do you want?"

"Good morning to you, too, Bro," Phil said.

"You're not my brother," Nick said.

"I am too. I had DNA run on the whole family two years ago. I never thought that one family could ever be this disturbed." Phil laughed.

Nick said, "Would you please get to the point. I have a terrible headache..."

"They're called hangovers," Phil said.

"Fine, have it your way," Nick said. "I have a hangover and I would like to crawl to the bathroom door and slam it on my head to see if it helps."

"Why don't you just take some aspirin?" Phil asked.

"Because, smart guy, aspirin can hurt your stomach," Nick said.

"And alcohol can't?" Phil asked.

"Why are you here?" Nick asked.

"I need to talk to you about Sinclair," Phil said.

Nick seemed to sober up immediately. "What about Sinclair?"

Phil explained that Sinclair wasn't sleeping, not eating and when he did sleep, he suffered from something like the night terrors.

"He's deteriorating before our eyes," Phil said. "Somethings going on with him; you need to talk to him."

"Why don't you talk to him?" Nick said.

"Because in the old days, if I brought up something like this to him he would have shot me. Now I'm afraid he wouldn't," Phil said. "Something is eating away at him."

"Okay, let me get showered and dismiss my suicidal thoughts and I will speak with him. Now, will you get out of my room?" Nick said.

"Gladly, and Nick," Phil said, "that shower is a great idea, you smell like a distillery."

"Get out of here because I will shoot you," Nick said.

+

Nick strolled into Sinclair's office and said, "Honey, you're scaring the children."

"You're a special kind of asshole, aren't you?" Sinclair replied.

"Not really," Nick said, "just a regular old Yankee asshole. Hey seriously, Phil and the young ladies are concerned about what they described as your bad dreams. You want to talk about it?"

"Why?" Sinclair asked. "What did you do, join the Universal Life church and now you are a confessor and spiritual counselor?"

"How did you know about that? You really are a detective," Nick said. "Sinclair, they are worried about you. You haven't been yourself."

There are two things Nick hoped he would never see. The first was seeing his dad, Billy, cry, and he saw that when his mother died and again when his granddaughter was killed. The second thing was to see tears in Sinclair's eyes.

"Sit down," Sinclair said.

Nick sat.

"I never told you or anyone everything about the night that Deidra died," Sinclair began. " I was working a case, an important case the night she disappeared. The rehearsal she went to was an open rehearsal. Barbeau did that kind of thing

93

every once in a while to keep the checks and donations from the parents rolling in. I was supposed to take her to the studio and stay for the rehearsal.

"Like I said, I was working a case. About a half hour before she had to go, I got a call about a lead on the case. I had her mother drive her and I said that I would swing by and pick her mother up and we would be there for the rehearsal. I got hung up, lost track of time and couldn't pick her mom up and I never made to the rehearsal. I never saw her alive again. The next time I saw her she was broken and being pulled out of a dumpster in an alley in the Quarter. I should have been there, I should have walked her into that dance studio that night. If I had, she might be alive."

Nick sat silent and didn't know what to say. He knew what his friend and mentor was feeling. He had asked himself similar questions when his daughter was killed. If he had only gotten home fifteen minutes earlier? If after he and his partner had taken seriously the threats made against them during an investigation, he had insisted that Annie, his ex-wife, had taken his daughter and gone to her family's home? If he had never gone into the family "business" and joined the Chicago Police Department? If he had listened to his brother Wil, a rising star in the CPD, and didn't take the case he was working in the first place. Nick knew all the questions, all the 'ifs' and all the pain and all the quilt of not being there when the ones that you loved needed you most.

"Nick, I'd like to be alone for a while."

Nick stood and walked to the door, when it opened, and Katie walked in.

"But Paw-Paw, you're not alone," she said. "She looked at Nick and said, "Neither are you. Greg and I were alone, no family, no future, no one who loved or cared for us. Then Nick and your family and your other family at the agency invited us into your lives. Now we have a family with two grandpas, you Sinclair and Billy, we have Pop, we have uncles and an aunt, all of you gave us that family. For the first time in either of our lives we felt like we belonged someplace. You lost Deidra tragically and no one can replace her ever, but you're not alone, you have a family of people who love you and look up to you, and who need you."

Katie began to cry and rushed from the room.

There was a deafening silence.

Sinclair looked up at Nick.

Nick shrugged his shoulders and quietly said, "What she said."

Chapter 26

Nick and Bart were sitting in a small meeting room on the third floor.

Cal entered and seemed preoccupied and then cleared his throat. "I'm glad you're both here."

"What's on your mind, Cal?" Bart asked.

"It's about last night," he said. "I would do anything for you guys. I will sweep the room or do all the interviews at the studio, but if it is okay with you, I would not like to be present when Bart..."

"Talks to dead people?" Nick said.

"Yes," said Cal.

"It is a little nerve-racking, isn't it," Bart said.

"I'd go so far as to say that its damned freaky," Nick said.

"That's okay, you don't have to be up there with us, but I would like you to be at the bottom of the stairs in case we need a reinforcement," Bart said.

"Reinforcement?" Cal asked.

"Yeah, in case we run into anything that isn't a spirit that we have trouble with," Nick said.

"I can do that," Cal said.

"Good," Nick said, "but we need to debrief each other about what happened or what we thought happened last night," Bart said.

"Do we," Nick said.

"You said, you wanted to debrief," Bart said.

"You're right. I'll start," Nick said.

"Be my guest," Bart said.

"I will," Nick replied. "We went to the studio's fifth floor. Bart communicated with a ghost. The ghost gave Bart his name, Peter Dawson. The ghost left or he opened and closed the door as we left. Does that about sum it up?"

"Yep," Bart said.

"We need to get back over there so Cal can sweep the room for tricks," Nick said. "We'd better take Greg with us this morning."

+

Cal started his sweep, he noticed something blinking in a heat vent. He climbed up to look at it. It appeared to be a tiny projector. He walked over to a floor vent where there was a small tube sticking up.

He looked at Nick. "I think someone has been playing games with us."

Then Cal waked over to some crates by the door and he found two audio speakers, "We have definitely been screwed with."

Nick, Bart, and Greg looked at each other.

Cal walked over to the door and found two very thin wires attached to the bottom of the door. "Uh huh," Cal said, "we've been fooled."

Nick looked at Bart, "Were you fooled?"

"I wasn't fooled," Bart said, "were you?"

"Nope," Nick said. "Greg, what did Cal miss?"

"Not much," Greg said, "just the two hoses blowing cold air and the lights."

Cal looked confused.

"Cal, I apologize for messing with you last night," Nick said, "but we had to see if someone who didn't believe in paranormal experience would buy in. We had Greg set this up. We have to repeat the show for Fontane who is a believer or Ti who isn't."

"Last night was a hoax?" Cal asked.

"Not all of it," Bart said."

"What part wasn't?" Cal asked.

"When Nick and you were bringing the equipment up from the van, I was up here doing my 'ghostie' thing and there is a presence here and I did communicate with one."

"Let me guess, Dawson," Cal said.

"I told you this guy was good," Nick said.

"All that I learned and what he told me was what I told you later," Bart said. "The rest was a show and misdirection."

"You know how, when we set up something like we did with the ladies in the Crowe case, we say something? What was the last thing I said to you before we put that operation into motion?"

Cal thought for a moment, then smiled. "The circus is in town."

"Yep, but this time, the carny was in town," Nick said. "It was a rehearsal for what we may have to do."

Cal laughed, "You two are really crazy assholes."

Nick laughed and said, "Well, yeah. Tonight, Bart and I will be back here, and Bart will try to connect with whatever or whoever is here."

"What do you want me to do?" Cal asked.

"We want you on the fourth floor making sure Bart isn't disturbed," Nick said. "We're going to meet with Fontane and Trip now. Katie and Alana should be here soon, and we would like the three of you to continue interviewing the staff and any dancers that are in the building, Oh, feel free to hint that there is indeed spiritual activity here."

Bart said, "You won't be lying."

Chapter 27

Bart and Nick walked up the administrative offices; Ti was standing in front of his Father's office.

"You two and the rest of your entourage are frauds," he said.

"Good morning to you, too," Nick said. "Sounds like someone should switch to decaf."

It sounded like Ti actually growled. "Don't think I don't know what your scam is."

"Scam?" Bart replied.

"What are you going to do, tell my father that you have found ghosts and for a fee you can get rid of them. I've seen your kind before," Ti said, "and I'm not going to allow you to take advantage of him."

"Good," Bart said, "because we are not going to take advantage of him." Bart turned to Nick and took a dollar bill out of his pocket and handed it to Nick. "You're right, you win, he really is as dumb as you said he was."

Ti moved towards Bart.

"No, no, no," Nick said, "step back..."

"What are you going to do about it?" Ti said.

"I'm going to give you some good advice," Nick said.

"Advice?" Ti said, looking confused and angry. "What would that be?"

"It's very simple," Nick said, "unless you want to do an imitation of a mop, mopping this floor in front of the staff, you will get out of the way, now," Nick said.

Ti smirked and said, "This floor is carpeted."

Nick looked at Bart and handed the dollar bill back to him. "Maybe he isn't as stupid as I thought he was."

"Don't know," Bart said, "he's still here."

The door to Fontane's office opened and Trip walked out. "Good, you're here, my grandfather is ready to see you."

Bart said, "Good, we won't keep him waiting," and entered the office followed by Nick.

Nick looked at Ti, and said, "This was fun, we should do it again. I won't keep you. I'm sure you have tutus to count or something, don't you?"

As Nick turned to enter the office and closed the door, he thought he heard another faint growl.

Fontane was sitting at his desk and looked anxious.

"Any news, did you find anything?" He asked.

"Yes, we did," Bart said. "There is definitely a presence here. Who it is or who they are we don't know, yet."

"Was it the girl?" Trip said.

"Perhaps," Bart said, "we need to investigate further."

"Your son is under the impression that we are collecting a fee for this," Nick said. "I assure you there is no fee. We are investigating because it is what we do. We haven't and we will not ever ask for a fee or for expenses. We are doing this to find the truth and further our research."

"Ti is very high strung and suspicious of everyone and everything," the old man said. "You are here because I want you here and this is my studio and not his, yet. You are also here because I believe my grandson has experienced something and I respect and trust him."

"We have your permission to proceed with our investigation?" Bart said.

"You have," Fontane said. "Could you tell me just a little of what you have found?"

"Yes," Bart said. "The presence we believe was someone who died in an accident here around the turn of the last century. We believe he was a workman of some type."

"You know the history of the building," Nick said. "From the period, say 1900 and 1905, was there any construction or renovation going on in the building?"

"That was before we owned the building. It was still a warehouse. From what I heard during that period there were fortifications done on what has become the fifth floor, on the roof and floors. It was an old building back then and mostly wood. It hadn't been kept up. There was a lot of new building

100

going on in New Orleans at that time. My guess is that the owners were trying to renovate for another use than a warehouse and they were smart. They started by strengthening the structure with stronger and more durable materials. All the floors were reconstructed at that time."

"Are you aware of any workman who may have died during this time working on the building?" Bart asked.

"I really don't know, but I imagine there could have been," Fontane said.

"We have some of our people looking into that," Nick said. "Of course, if we find anything we will pass it on. We are also looking into those who have died that had a connection with your studio."

"I am aware that there have been, tragically, some of our students who passed on in this area since we have been operating, but none of them died in this building," Fontane said.

"If none of them died here," Trip said, "then why do you think I saw the woman in our building?"

"There could be many reasons," Bart said. "That's what we will try to find out."

"We won't take any more of your time and thank you for helping us with this. The information you have given us will help," Bart said.

As Bart and Nick got up to leave, Fontane said to Bart, "You should give Mr. Neff his dollar back. My son is just as dumb as you think he is."

Nick and Bart smiled and nodded and left Fontane's office.

"What should we do now?" Bart asked.

"Let's check in with Casey and Phil. They may have found out something about our Mr. Dawson," Nick said.

"I think I will go up to the fifth floor," Bart said.

"Why?" Nick asked, "we're coming back tonight."

Bart smiled and said, "To understand the living, you've got to commune with the dead." It was the worst imitation of Ima P. Hall's character, Minerva, in *Midnight in the Garden of Good and Evil,* that Nick had ever heard.

Nick looked at him, "Okay then, see you later."

Chapter 28

Phil spent the morning researching city and parish records. He walked into the ballroom where Casey was searching for records online about construction and Dawson.

"How did it go?" Casey asked.

"Well, almost every year since they have been keeping records, something has been worked on at that address," Phil said. "And from 1903–1905 are the years that the fourth and fifth floor looks were built."

"What was it like prior to that?" Casey asked.

"I looked at the plans for the building that I had gotten before from the city. It looks like the exterior walls were always tall enough for a five-story building, but the top two floors weren't built until the beginning of the twentieth century. What's really kind of interesting is that when Barbeau took over the building the fifth floor was left intact but half of floors two, three and four were removed. You want to guess why?"

"Sure," Casey said. "The Barbeau Group removed half of three floors to create what will be a revolutionary performance space, dressing rooms, green room and wing space."

"Good guess," Phil said.

"Not a guess, sonny, fact. I read an article on it," Casey said.

"Where did you find that?" Phil asked.

"I found an old article in a theatre magazine about converting nontraditional spaces into performance spaces," she said. "The article cited Barbeau's warehouse in the article as 'Going Big' as opposed to the usual nontraditional spaces that were converted into performance spaces like lofts, storefronts or even old gas stations."

"That sounds pretty cool," Phil said. "When is Nick getting back?"

"He's on his way now," Casey said.

"So how is it going," Phil asked.

"What do you mean?" Casey said.

A voice from the doorway said, "He means that everybody, including Baron and Ruby are aware of how you look at him." The voice was Sinclair.

"I don't know what you're talking about?" Casey said.

"Really?" Sinclair said. "What about that Baron?"

Baron looked up and if a dog could roll his eyes, Baron did.

"Would you like some advice from an old man?" Sinclair said.

"No," Casey said.

"Good, I am going to give you some anyway," Sinclair said.

"Wonderful," she said.

"Casey, I think Nick is interested in you and has been since we did the case in St. Louis. Also, I think that he is considering moving the cold case operation to St. Louis because of that interest in you," Sinclair said. "He may not know that's why he is doing it, but I think that is why. He wants a fresh start and I think he is tired of being by himself."

Baron and Ruby raised their heads.

Sinclair looked at them. "Calm down, I know you too are with him, but he needs to have humans too."

They laid their heads down and Ruby groaned.

"What do you think, Phil?" Sinclair said, "and no smartass comments right now."

Phil smiled. "The old man is right and if you're waiting for him to make his move, you'll be waiting and waiting and waiting. Now can I give a smartass comment?"

Sinclair sighed. "If you must."

"I think," Phil said, "you should go to dinner at a romantic restaurant in the Quarter, get him sloppy drunk, throw him over your shoulder and have your way with him."

"You know, son, you were born without any sense and are devoid of the genes associated with any kind of class," Sinclair said.

Phil smiled. "Thank you."

"Remember, Casey, she who hesitates is lost," Sinclair said.

"Well, Dear Abby, are you and Ann Landers done?" Casey said.

"Yes," Sinclair said.

"I think you should probably mind your own business," Casey said.

"Spoken like a woman who is destined to live alone with twenty cats," Phil said.

A book flew past Phil's head.

"Missed," he said.

"Missed what?" Nick said, coming through the door.

"Casey threw a book at Phil," Sinclair said.

Nick looked at Casey and said, "You missed?" He picked up a stapler. "Here, try this."

Phil got behind a file cabinet.

"So, if we are done with recess, can we get back to work?" Nick said.

"I guess that's my cue to leave," Sinclair said.

"No, you need to be part of this," Nick said, "but no shooting the suspects...yet. Can you do that?"

"I can try," Sinclair said.

Nick updated them on the encounter with Ti, and the meeting with Fontane and Trip. Casey and Phil updated him on what they had found.

When they were finished Nick asked if he could have the room to talk to Sinclair. Casey and Phil went to the kitchen to have lunch.

"Are you going to ask me to swear that I won't shoot anyone?"

"Not yet, but I need you back on this case as a detective, not as a dad," Nick said.

"Okay, I can try," he said.

"I know you're skeptical about these things, but Bart thinks there is something going on at the studio."

"Spirits?" Sinclair asked. "I'm not that skeptical. I live with a ghost."

"Don't we all," Nick said, with a smile.

"I am coming up with a different theory about the case," Nick said. "I would like to talk to you about it when I get back from the studio this evening."

"Fine, I'm not sleeping much anyway," Sinclair said.

"Good, there are some things I want to check out tonight," Nick said.

"Do you mind if I make a suggestion?" Sinclair asked.

"Would it matter if I did?" Nick said, smiling.

"No," Sinclair said.

"What's your suggestion?" Nick asked.

"You have put a lot of responsibility on Casey," Sinclair said. "She is managing all the research and the staff. She is debriefing the staff every day and she hasn't left the house since we went to O'Brien's. She is going to burn out."

"What do you suggest?" Nick asked.

"I know that there are some things about the case she is concerned about, and she wants to talk to you about," Sinclair said.

"Okay, I can speak to her before I go back to the studio tonight," Nick said.

"I was thinking that maybe tonight or tomorrow night you two could get out of here and go to some place quiet and have dinner, "Sinclair said. "Nick, it's no secret that if you do decide to set up the cold case shop in St. Louis, she is going to be in charge of the administration of the St. Louis office. You don't want to risk burning her out. You are going to need her, and she is loyal not only to Caldwell and Cheswick Investigations, but she is loyal to you."

"Okay, do you have an idea where she might like to go?" Nick asked.

"I do, there is a nice place on Bourbon Street called Galatoire's," Sinclair said.

"Do you know anyone over there that can get a table for us?" Nick said.

Sinclair said, "I do, and I will take care of it. I'll make it for tomorrow night."

"Thanks, and I'll see you later this evening," Nick said. "I have to get back over to the studio."

Nick walked out as Phil walked into the ballroom.

"Oh, Phil, can you put a six pack of the pictures of the five women that we know died and get it to me at the studio this afternoon?" Nick asked.

Phil said, "Sure," I'll put it together and get it over there by three."

"See you later," Nick said.

Phil looked at Sinclair and said, "Well?"

"They're going to dinner tomorrow night," Sinclair said, with a smile.

"You're a sneaky old man," Phil said.

"I am," Sinclair said, "Yes, I am."

Chapter 29

Trip sat in the conference room waiting for Nick to arrive.

"Thank you for meeting me," Nick said.

"My grandfather said that you wanted to talk to me about what I saw that night in the studio."

"I do," Nick said.

"You don't think I'm crazy, do you?" Trip asked.

"No, I don't. Do you think you're crazy?" Nick asked.

"No, I know what I saw, and it scared the hell out of me," Trip answered.

"That would be an appropriate response, I think," Nick said. "Trip, we have put together what we call a six pack of photos for you to look at. These photos are the women that we know had a connection with the studio and have also gone missing or met with an untimely death. I would like you to look at these photos and tell me if you recognize the woman that you saw that night. Are you willing to do that for me?"

Trip got very quiet, then said, "She looked so sad, I had never seen anyone look that sad."

"I'm sorry that it upset you but maybe if you look at the photos and can point the woman out if she is in these pictures and we can identify her, it might help you," Nick said.

"How," Trip asked.

"You will learn her name and it will confirm that you saw someone who actually existed. And if you have any doubt about what you saw being real, it might clear up any question about your experience being real," Nick said.

"Can I see the pictures?" Trip said.

Nick placed the pictures on the table.

"Now, Trip, look at the pictures, take your time and tell me if the person you saw is in this group," Nick said.

Trip looked at the photographs.

There was a knock at the door and Bart stuck his head in. "Am I interrupting anything?"

"No," Nick said, "Trip is looking at the photographs."

It was clear that he was focusing on one photograph in particular. Nick and Bart noticed that he was clearly upset.

Do you recognize any of them?" Bart asked.

Trip looked at Bart and he looked as if he were on the verge of tears. He pointed to a picture. "It was her," he said quietly, "my God it was her."

Nick looked at the picture. "You are sure that this is the woman that followed you into the studio and walked up the staircase?"

"Yes, but in the picture, she looks happy," Trip said.

"Thank you, Trip, we're going to do a little more investigating and when we finish, I promise you that I will give you and your grandfather all the information we have," Nick said.

Trip looked at Nick, clearly shaken, and almost whispered, "Would it be all right for me to go back to my office?"

"Go ahead, I know this was hard, but you did fine," Nick said.

Trip rose and left the room.

Nick sat down at the table and Bart sat across from him. They both looked at the picture that trip picked out of the six photographs.

"Surprised," Bart asked.

"No, are you?" Nick said.

"Not really," Bart said.

"I think we need to keep this between us for a while," Nick said.

"Agreed," Bart said, "particularly when we get back to the rest of the crew."

They sat in silence. There was a shared sadness as they looked at the picture of Deidra Sinclair smiling at them.

Chapter 30

Bart asked, "What are you thinking?"

Nick and Bart were sitting on an old couch on the fifth floor of the studio, waiting.

"I don't know," Nick said, "I guess I'm trying to figure out if I were in Sinclair's position if I would want to know that my daughter's spirit had appeared to someone."

"Well?" Bart asked.

"I'm not sure," Nick said. "If I knew, I would probably want to storm in here and wait to see if I could catch a glimpse of her one more time."

"That probably would not be a good thing for the investigation," Bart said.

"No, that would probably end the investigation and God knows what Sinclair would do," Nick said.

"If she reveals herself to us I could ask her," Bart said.

Nick looked at him.

"There is a chance," Bart said.

Nick remained silent.

"This is difficult for you, I know. You don't really believe, do you?" Bart asked.

"I believe you believe. I believe that when you have investigated things like this you have received information that has helped us solve cases. I want to believe," Nick said. "I want to believe that there is something more than this, that in some way we continue. I want to believe someday I will see Mary again and my son Wil, I want to believe that I will see my mom, I want to believe that I will see Duke, I want to believe that I can believe."

"But you don't," Bart said.

Nick looked at the floor.

"Your father should have named you Thomas," Bart smiled.

Nick smiled. "Thomas would have made a great detective; he was a fact and evidence guy. He wanted verification, he would have probably looked for the rocks in the sea and verified the walking on water and checked if there were kegs of wine hidden away at the wedding at Cana."

"Do you think he would have called for an autopsy too?" Bart asked, with a smile.

Nick got up from the couch and walked over to a space heater they had brought up and turned it up. "It's getting a little chilly in here."

"It is," Bart said.

Then Nick walked to the corners of the room to make sure the cool air tubes that had been installed by Greg weren't blowing cool air. They weren't.

Bart got up and surveyed the room, then sat on an old beat-up chair that had been stored up on the fifth floor, probably for years.

"It's after midnight, why don't you take a nap on the couch, you look tired," Bart said.

"No, I'll wait up with you to see if anything happens," Nick said. He flopped back on the couch and within ten minutes he was out like a light.

After a few minutes, Nick woke up, and looked around and Bart was nowhere to be found.

"Bart?" he called, but there was no answer. He got up from the couch and called again. He pulled his Glock from his holster and walked toward the door, and he heard a voice behind him.

"Mr. Caldwell, or do you want me to call you Professor Neff? I don't think you will need that," the voice said calmly.

He turned and a young woman was sitting on the couch. It was Deidra Sinclair.

Nick said nothing.

"Mr. Cardwell then. I heard your conversation with Mr. Cheswick, and I know this must be hard for you," she said. "I know that you are here because of your devotion to my father."

Nick struggled to speak. "Who's your father?"

She giggled. "You want me to verify that I am who you know I am?"

"Answer the question," Nick said.

"My father is Sinclair Stewart. He is a detective and your friend. You remind me of him. You are a 'just the facts' kind of guy, like he is," she said. "You are here because you are investigating the women who have disappeared or were found murdered that had a connection with the studio, but you are really here to find out who murdered me. How am I doing?"

"So, you are a ghost?" Nick said.

"I don't really know what I am," she said, "but I know that I don't live in your world. Besides, how can I be a ghost, you don't believe in ghosts and spirits, do you?" she said with a smile, "but here I am and here you are."

"You're a smart-aleck like your old man," Nick said.

"I will take that as a compliment," she said.

"It was meant as one," Nick said. "Why are you appearing to me?"

"Because you care about my dad as much as you care about your own and I think my father thinks of you as a son," she said, "and I can help you."

"Why did you appear to Trip Barbeau?" Nick asked.

"Because," she said, "he has a good heart, and he believes, and I knew that he would support his grandfather's wish to find out who is living up here, well not exactly living. I knew eventually that if the person that killed me and the others was to be brought to justice, it would take you to find them."

"Why didn't you just appear to your father? He believes," Nick said.

She smiled. "If I had told my dad, he would have come here and probably shot someone, don't you agree?"

Nick gave her a little smile. "I do."

"He is usually a facts and evidence guy like you, but in this situation, I think it might have ended up in a shoot first and ask questions later," she said.

112

"Deidra, who murdered you?" Nick asked.

"I can't tell you that, Mr. Caldwell," she said.

"Why not?" Nick asked.

"Because you need to find evidence so that he can be brought to justice," she said, "and, because, you already know, don't you?"

"I have my suspicions," Nick said.

"I know you do, but you need to look deeper." She smiled.

"What do you mean, look deeper?" Nick said.

Deidra smiled at him. "What don't you understand. I don't think you are the kind of detective that is satisfied with the obvious answer. You're not that kind of detective, are you, Mr. Caldwell?"

"Okay, I get your point. How would you suggest that I get the evidence to bring this person or persons to justice?" Nick asked.

"The box," she said.

"The box?" Nick asked.

"Yes, the box," she said.

"What box?" Nick asked.

"The box that he keeps his souvenirs in. He has my locket in that box," she said. "I don't know where it is but probably somewhere close, by the way he reacted when you first came here...."

"It is probably somewhere up here or somewhere in the building, maybe the cellar," Nick said to himself.

"Mr. Caldwell, it's time for me to go, but when you solve this, would you tell my father that my mother and I are all right, and we love him very much. When you solve this we will be at peace, and we will be waiting for him when it is his time."

"I will," Nick promised.

"Nick, Nick, wake up," Bart said, "time to go."

Nick opened his eyes and looked around.

"It's half past three, time to get back to Sinclair's," Bart said.

"She was here," Nick said.

"Who?" Bart asked.

"Deidra, she was here," Nick said. "I fell asleep, and I woke up and you weren't here but..."

"Nick, I haven't left this room, except to go get coffee and go to the john. I was only gone for a few minutes. It was a dream. I did notice you were a little restless..."

"She was here," Nick said firmly, "and she gave me a lead."

"Okay, what is the lead?" Bart asked.

"A box, the son of a bitch keeps souvenirs," Nick said. "It's hidden somewhere in the building, probably up here or it could be in the cellar. Her locket is in it. We find the box, we got him."

"Then we look for the box," Bart said, "but now, let's go back and get some rest. In the morning we can plan how to find it and how we can make sure we can connect it to the murderer."

"We are going to need the murderer to check the box and we catch him with it," Nick said. "We are going to need Greg and Cal to set up surveillance cameras up here and in other areas that are used often in the building. We have to keep this between the four of us."

"We can start on this in the morning, let's go," Bart said.

They walked toward the door and Nick turned to Bart and said, "She was here."

Bart smiled. "Nick, I believe you."

Chapter 31

"You look like hell," Bart said as Nick sat down for breakfast.

"And good morning to you too," Nick replied.

"Sleep well?" Bart asked.

"What do you think," Nick said.

"Well, you should be rested," Bart said. "After all you did have a nap last night at the studio."

Nick raised his eyebrow. "You're enjoying this, aren't you?"

Bart smiled. "Oh, yeah."

"It was a dream," Nick said.

"I didn't say it wasn't," Bart said.

"I had a dream, that's all," Nick insisted.

"So, you're not a believer?" Bart asked.

"I believe in facts and evidence," Nick said.

"If you say so," Bart said. "What is the plan for today."

"I think we need to have another conversation with Fontane about the renovations particularly about what has been done on the fifth floor and cellar," Nick said.

"Following a lead from nap time, I see." Bart laughed.

"Listen, I had a dream. It only makes sense that whoever killed these women would keep trophies; most of these sick bastards do," Nick said. "It's also clear that they had some kind of connection with the studio. Even though we can't prove it, I'm guessing Felix will find that something happened on the fifth floor, and maybe the cellar."

"Okay, Caldwell, what's going on?"

"What do you mean?" Nick asked.

"I know that look, there is something bothering you, what is it?" Bart asked.

"I'm having trouble with the main suspect," Nick said.

Bart looked surprised, "Why?"

"I think we...I think I jumped to a conclusion because the guy is a raving lunatic. You were a shrink. This Ti has little or no self-control, do you really think he could do something like this and pull it off for all these years?" Nick asked.

Bart thought for a minute. "Maybe, I see your point, but what are you getting at? Are you thinking the old man is involved?"

"No, I don't think that Fontane had anything to do with this," Nick said.

"Then what?" Bart asked.

"I looked at the studio employee list when we got back here," Nick said. "I couldn't sleep, I started thinking and I got a feeling that we need to look deeper. When I looked at the employee list, I saw there are eleven people who have been employed at the studio during the time these murders and disappearances took place. There are four women and seven men. Fontane and TI are in that group, so that leaves five men that we haven't really investigated."

"What is the age range of the five men?" Bart asked.

"That's the thing, they all are about the same age of Ti," Nick said.

That's what got me thinking. You would think that there might be an older guy in the group, but they are all in their forties," Nick said.

"They were all in their late twenties and thirties," Bart said.

"Correct," Nick said.

"What are you getting at? Are you saying that maybe Ti wasn't involved?" Bart asked.

"No, not at all," Nick said. "I'm just suggesting that maybe we have to give these guys a good look."

"How do we want to do this without arousing suspicion?" Bart said. "Katie and Cal have conducted several interviews already."

"I know, but they have been doing interviews about if has anyone seen or heard anything that goes bump in the night," Nick said. "This time we interview all eleven who were around at the time of the murders. This time we ask this group about if they remember the victims under the guise that we are trying find out who our 'ghosts' are. I know it's a long shot, but maybe someone will slip up and we'll get lucky."

Bart thought for a minute. "Who should do the interviews? I don't think it should be you or me."

"I agree, I think Katie should interview the women, and they may remember the victims. I think we divide the guys' interviews between Cal and Greg."

"Greg?" Bart said.

"He's licensed now," Nick said.

"In Illinois," Bart said. "You think he's ready for something like this?"

"I do, Felix has trained him to question everything, and he has sat in on several of these kinds of interviews and he has been around here and is a familiar face," Nick said.

"It's your call," Bart said.

"I want to ask for a favor," Nick said.

"You're going to ask? Are you feeling okay?" Bart said.

"Funny," Nick said.

"I thought so," Bart said. "What's the favor?"

"Would it be possible for Constance to get away and come down?" Nick asked.

"You want Trebble down here?" Bart said.

"Yeah, and maybe my brother-in-law," Nick said.

"You want Constance and Bob Wilson...down here?" Bart said.

"Uh-huh," Nick said.

"Can I ask why?" Bart asked.

"Yes, you may," Nick said. There was silence.

"Well?" Then Bart shook his head. "You're a jerk sometimes."

"Sometimes?" Nick replied.

"Okay," Bart said, "why do you want them down here?"

"Thank you for asking. I want them down here because I want them to do surveillance on the five guys with Casey and Phil," Nick replied. "I need people that they won't recognize."

117

"Okay, I'll make the call before we go to the studio," Bart said, "but don't you need five people to surveil five people?"

"That is why we have been business partners all these years, nothing gets past you," Nick said.

Bart flipped Nick off.

Nick laughed. "And all these years everyone thought that you were the classy one."

"I am," Bart said, "who's the fifth?"

"I have someone local in mind," Nick said.

"Local, who?" Bart asked.

"Sinclair," Nick said.

"Are you crazy?" Bart said.

"Why, yes I am, "Nick replied, smiling.

"You don't think he may be a little too close to this case? Besides, one of these guys could recognize him," Bart said.

"I know," Nick said, "I'm sure they might. He's been a fixture in the Quarter since he was a cop, and he always makes people a little nervous when he is around. I'm going to have our five rotate the surveillance on the other five."

"Are you sure about this?" Bart asked.

"Do you know anyone that is a better investigator than him? I don't. I'm also bringing someone else in," Nick said.

"What?" Bart said, "Who?"

"I can't say, now," Nick said, "but I will, I promise."

Sinclair walked into the dining room with a pot of coffee. "You two are up early, have you eaten?"

"Not yet," Nick said.

"Well, breakfast will be ready soon; do you mind if I join you?" Sinclair said, with a hint of sarcasm.

"Why not," Nick said.

"You look like crap," Sinclair said. "Didn't you sleep well?"

"No, I didn't, how about you?" Nick asked.

"Actually, I did get a little rest, I even dreamed for the first time in a long time."

Bart filled his coffee cup and asked, "What did you dream about?"

"I dreamed about Deidra," he said.

"I hope it was a good dream," Nick said.

"It's not unusual to have a dream about a loved one we have lost," Bart said.

"When I do dream, I usually dream about her and her mother," Sinclair said.

"Do you remember the dream?" Nick asked.

"Yes, I do," Sinclair said. "Usually, I just see her, and her presence is so real, I feel like she is still here, but last night's dream was different."

"How?" Nick asked.

"She was talking to you, Nick," Sinclair said, "Deidra was talking to you."

Chapter 32

M s. Johnson," Katie said.
"Please dear, Call me Ava."

"All right, Ava, you are the costumer for the studio, correct?" Katie asked.

"I am the costume designer," Ava replied.

"How long have you been with the studio?"

"For almost twenty-five years," Ava replied. "Most of the production staff has been here that long."

Katie continued, "You are aware why we are here, and what we are investigating, I suppose."

"My understanding is that you are investigating paranormal activity at the request of Fontane," Ava said, smiling.

"That's correct. In your time here have you experienced anything that you would consider paranormal activity?" Katie asked.

"You mean have I seen any ghosts?" Ava asked. "No, I haven't, but every theatre has ghosts."

"Have you witnessed anything that you consider could be perhaps spirit activity?" Katie asked.

"If you mean bumps in the night, strange sounds, that sort of thing, then yes, I have," Ava said. "Theatres can be creepy places at night, particularly in an old building, but do I believe that there are spirits roaming the halls, no. The building, as I said, is very old, so there are bound to be odd noises in a building like this."

"Are you aware of any deaths that may have occurred here?" Katie asked.

"Of course," Ava said. "There are several stories of workmen and people who worked here and died here when it was a warehouse before the studio was founded. I think it would be difficult for a building as old as this not to have had some people pass on. I don't think you could find any building this old in New Orleans that hasn't had someone die in it." She smiled. "This is an old community with a very volatile and colorful history."

"Are you aware that several young women who had a connection to the studio as students or members of the master company have either died or gone missing over the last twenty-five years?"

Ava's smile faded. "I am, but none of them died in this building," she said firmly.

"That's true," Katie said, "but it seems odd that so many have met troubling ends over the years."

"We are located in one of the most beautiful and at times dangerous parts of the city," she said.

"So, you're saying, regarding these missing and dead young women, your answer is 'shit happens' in the Quarter?" Katie asked, not looking up as she wrote.

At that moment Ms. Ava Johnson realized that she may have underestimated little Ms. Katie.

"I wouldn't characterize what I said quite like that," Ava objected.

Katie smiled. "Okay, may I ask you another question?"

Ava had a look on her face as if she was having a root canal without nova cane. "Yes," she said, tentatively.

"Did you know any of the women who were victims or went missing?" Katie asked.

"Why are you asking me that?" Ava asked.

Katie replied, "Well, we have discovered that there are some who work here or have worked here who have seen spirits of young women on the fifth floor…"

"I never go on the fifth floor," Ava said.

"Oh, in all the years you have worked here. you have never gone on the fifth floor?" Katie said.

"No, it has always creeped me out," Ava blurted out.

"Why's that?" Katie asked.

"I don't know, it just does," Ava said. "Are we almost done here?"

"Just a couple more questions." Katie smiled.

"Do you ever go to the basements, either the first basement or the sub-basement?"

Ava looked upset. "Rarely. We do store costumes and sets down there."

"Okay, did you remember or know Holley Massey, Ashlyn Hodges, Eliza Allen, Denise Lawson, Amanda Lee or Deidra Stewart?" Katie asked.

"If they came through the studio, I probably met them," Ave said.

"Are you aware of any one here who may have had a closer relationship with these women?" Katie asked.

"I really have to go; I have fittings scheduled for today," Ava said.

"I won't keep you any longer, I think I have everything I may need," Katie said, smiling

A much paler Ava Johnson rushed from the room.

Chapter 33

Cal extended his hand and asked, "Mr. Moreau, I'm Alphonse Calvin with the paranormal group from the university, but you can call me Al."

René Moreau was a small man, a nervous type. He took Cal's hand and gave it a light shake. "You may call me René."

"Please sit, René," Cal said. "I have been told that you are the musical director and a choreographer for the studio."

"Yes, I have had the honor of working for Maestro Fontane for twenty-seven years," René said.

"I bet you have seen a lot of talented young dancers come through here," Cal said.

"I have and it has been my task to develop that talent," René said, "when I am not interfered with."

"Interfered with?" Cal said. "Let me guess, are you referring to Ti?"

"I didn't say that," René said, "but yes, and that … never mind."

Cal smiled. "And who else?"

"I'd rather not say," René said. "Besides, he is an idiot, knows nothing about the arts, he is a hack, but he has the ear of the Maestro's son, they were childhood friends. He is a classic bore. Just because he can manipulate the press, he is a hero."

"Do you mean Jasper Marchal?" Cal asked.

"You've met him?" René asked.

"I have," Cal said.

"He is a buffoon and a letch," René said. "He would appear at the rehearsals saying he needed to see the program so he could properly promote the *danse d 'école*. The fool didn't even speak French. He came to drool over the dancers. He did it for years and still does. I complained to the Maestro, who told him to cease. Ti told him he could continue to be at the rehearsals, and he told him if there was a problem to report it to him immediately. Jasper would have interviews with my dancers for program notes. Many of the young ladies were upset after meeting with him. When I would ask them why they were upset, they wouldn't say. These were young women. When I would ask them why they were upset, they were silent."

"Did you report this to Ti?" Cal asked.

"I did. I demanded that there be a chaperone in those meetings," René said.

"Did Ti take any action?" Cal asked.

"No," René said. "I do not think I should say anymore."

"René, it's okay. Anything you say to me will stay with me," Cal assured him.

René was silent for a moment, then said, "Alphonse, are you aware of Ti's temper?"

"I understand that he and Professor Neff and Bartholomew have had a run in with him," Cal said.

"I heard. He is an abusive person," René said.

"René, has he ever threatened you?" Cal asked.

"Always, most of us who work here are..." René stopped.

Cal finished his sentence, "Have been intimidated by him."

"Yes," René said. "What he does behind the Maestro's back is disturbing. We're all nervous about what will happen to the studio and our careers when he takes over."

"René, you didn't finish telling me what happened after you demanded that a chaperone be present when the dancers met with Jasper," Cal said.

"There was a chaperone in those interviews," René said.

"Who was the chaperone?" Cal asked.

René looked down and said softly, "Ti."

Cal asked, "He would chaperone after you complained?"

"No, he had been in all the interviews with Jasper and the dancers, and still is in those interviews," René said.

They were both silent for a moment.

"You are very protective of your dancers, aren't you, René?"

"Yes, they are children on the edge of becoming young women," René said. "I tried to get them to come forward, but none were willing to. They were afraid and they wanted to continue with the company, and they had dreams of being professional dancers."

Cal said, "Would you mind if I asked you one more question?"

"No," René said. He seemed relieved that he finally had told his story to someone.

Cal handed him a list and pictures of the missing and murdered women. "René, were any of these women interviewed by Jasper and Ti, and were any of them upset about those interviews?"

124

René looked at the list, then the pictures, and tears welled up in his eyes.

"It's okay, René." Cal handed him a tissue.

Rene looked up. "All of them."

"Thank you, René," Cal said.

Cal was surprised when René asked, "Alphonse, aren't you going to ask me about the spirits?"

"Yes, I was getting to that," Cal lied. "Have you experienced any paranormal activity?"

René said sadly, "Yes." He handed Cal one of the pictures. "She regularly visits me."

"When was the last time she visited you?" Cal asked.

René looked up with tears running down his cheeks. "She visited me last night after the rehearsal and told me that when I had my interview with the paranormal team, I should tell you what I knew. She said she had already spoken with Nick. I checked this morning and realized that Dr. Neff's name is Nicholas. I have never talked about her visits to anyone."

"You have done the right thing, René," Cal said.

"Alphonse, may I go now?" René asked.

"Certainly, and I will inform Dr. Neff of our conversation and what you have shared will be confidential, I promise."

"Thank you, Alphonse," René said. He stood up and shook Cal's hand, this time with a firm handshake, and left the room.

Cal looked at the picture of the spirit that had been visiting René. It was Deidra Stewart. He sat alone in the room and said to himself and smiled, "Thank you, Deidra."

Chapter 34

Nick's cell began to buzz. "Yeah," he said.

"It's Phil, Bobby and Constance have arrived."

"Okay, we'll wrap it up here and head back. Tell everyone that after dinner we'll meet and go over Katie's and Cal's interviews. I also need to talk to Sinclair."

"Good, he wants to talk to you too," Phil said.

"Do you know what about?" Nick asked.

"Yes, I do," Phil said.

"I don't want him in that meeting tonight. I'll talk to him after the meeting," Nick said.

"Nick, it's not about the case," Phil said.

"Then what," Nick asked.

"It is something about that reservation that was made for you at a restaurant in the Quarter for you and the fair Casey that you didn't follow up on," Phil said. "You know it doesn't make Uncle Sinclair happy when he is disappointed. He starts cleaning his guns."

"Who in the hell made him Cupid?" Nick said.

"Even the suggestion of Sinclair in a Cupid costume is an image that will be hard to get out of my mind for weeks," Phil said. "I'll tell him you will talk to him after the meeting tonight."

"Fine," Nick said.

+

Nick and Bart sat at the long table in the ballroom that had been converted into the headquarters for the investigation as the rest of the team filed in. Casey sat at the end of the table flanked by Alana and Katie; Cal and Greg sat across from Phil and Felix with Bob Wilson and Constance Trebble, who had arrived from Chicago earlier in the day sitting across from each other.

The case board was behind Nick and a projection screen behind Bart. On the case Board there were pictures of the now seven known victims that were dead or missing that had connections to the Barbeau Studio. The seventh victim was Mindy Deleon, seventeen, found murdered in the Quarter five years ago.

The projection screen had the photos of the nine staff members that Cal and Katie interviewed that day.

"I'd like to begin by going over the interviews that Katie and Cal did today," Nick said. "Katie, why don't you begin."

"I spoke with Megan Thompson, one of the choreographers, Kathy Butler, the makeup artist, Julia Morris, the assistant costumer, and Ava Johnson, the costumer and designer. All four women have been with the studio for over twenty years," Katie said. "They all have one other thing in common; they all became nervous when I talked to them about Ti."

"Nervous in what way?" Bart asked.

"Well, Thompson, Butler and Morris clearly don't like the guy, but they love Fontane and Trip. Butler said, 'Maybe they would catch a break and Ti would get hit by a trolley and Trip would take over when his grandfather retired.' The others didn't comment a lot, but this guy has few friends," Katie said.

"Oh, I don't know, I found him to be quite pleasant," Nick said.

"Right," Cal laughed, "after you were standing over him when he 'tripped' and fell on the floor."

"Our legal staff thanks you, Cal, for your observation of that event," Bart said. "Go on, Katie."

"I interviewed the head costumer and designer, Ava Thompson. She's tough and seems to have been around. She has been there longer than the others. She is devoted to Fontane," Katie said, "but she was weird when we talked about Ti. It was like she was protective and at the same time fearful of him. There's something going on there. I'm going to snoop around a little more."

"You know, Katie, we never snoop, we investigate," Nick said.

"Yes, Daddy," she countered.

Everyone laughed. This exchange was common between Nick and Katie. They may not have been related by blood, but he was the only father figure she or Greg had ever really known.

"Cal, what did the gentlemen have to say," Bart asked.

"Next time can I interview the ladies?" Cal said, which got him a stern look from Alana.

"You're in trouble now," Nick said.

"Only kidding, my sweet," Cal said to Alana.

She smiled and ran her figure across her neck and smiled and pointed at him. The team laughed again.

"I think it is best that I continue," Cal said. "I interviewed Frank Moore, the lighting designer, Oscar Russo, set designer, Tomas Santos, the stage manager, Jasper Marchal, the public relations and marketing guy, what a piece of work this guy is, and the guy I learned the most from was René Moreau. He is a choreographer and the music director."

"What was it about Marchal that bothered you?" Bart asked.

"The guy is a sleezy creep. I Interviewed him in his office which has a front class wall," Cal said. "One of the ballet classes let out and the young girls walked by and all he could do was watch them walk by. I thought he was going to lick his lips; the guy has perve tendencies. He tried to control the interview by telling me that he made it all happen with his PR and marketing skills and that he and Ti went way back. The capper was when I showed him the pictures of the victims. He got this hint of little smile on his face, and I thought he was going to start panting. He looked like that old wolf character in the old cartoons whose eyes got big and screamed 'Ahoooga,' when Little Red Riding Hood walked by."

"Watching a lot of Cartoon Channel these days, are you, Cal?" Phil said.

"Yeah, with you, Philly," Cal said, with a smile.

"What did he say about the victims?" Nick asked.

"Nothing really," Cal said. "He said they looked familiar. Now this guy runs the media for the studio, there have been articles on all these girls, that would have been something he would have to do a spin on to protect the studio, and he says they look familiar."

"Good point," Nick said. "What about the others?"

"All the other guys indicated that they remembered most of them," Cal said, "but the room went silent after that. I checked around and all these guys had known Ti before they went to work there. They had gone either to high school or college with him."

"Do you think any of them could have been involved?" Nick asked.

"Involved?" Cal said. "I don't know, but I would bet if there was anything going on they may have known something about it. They were all hesitant to talk about Ti and were not eager to talk about Jasper either. It was weird."

"Casey, you and Phil do a little digging into Marchal," Nick said.

"Do you think Marchal could be involved with Ti in all this?" Casey asked.

"I think to transport a body might take two people," Nick said. I am glad that Bob and Constance are here, you've been listening, looking at the files, looking at the pictures, any initial reactions?"

Bob answered, "We do. We have looked at the files and I'm sure you have noticed the similarity in these girl's backgrounds. They all come from stable family environments, educational backgrounds are similar too, but Constance noticed something. Constance…"

"When we got here was the first time I looked at the photos. Then I began going through their files looking at their physical characteristics," Constance said. "I didn't have a lot of time but if you look at their height, weight, skin tone, hair color and facial structure, they could be sisters or at least cousins or relatives."

"A couple of those girls have blonde hair," Alana said.

"I know," Constance said, "but the two that have blond hair, were autopsied and there was an indication and evidence that chemicals associated with lightening hair were present. Our perp or perps may have a type."

"Good work," Nick said. "Cal and Katie, you do some digging on the folks you talked to. Cal, there was one more interview you did, right?"

"Yeah, I interviewed René Moreau, the music director, and he also choreographs some of the numbers. He has been here for years just like the others and has a fierce loyalty to Fontane and just as fierce a disgust of Ti and Jasper. He told me a lot about Ti and Jasper and their fixation on the young dancers. He did stand up for the girls and demanded that when interviewed by Jasper there be a chaperone present. Unfortunately, the chaperone was Ti. He is tougher than he seems, but I think he has been threatened by Jasper or Ti or both. Many of the women have sought him out to talk about this, but he said they were not ready to leave the company. He implied that some were putting the dream of a career ahead of their safety.

"When he saw Deidra's picture he was visibly moved. He also said that she visited him sometimes."

Bart looked at Nick.

"Did he say why she visited him?" Bart asked.

"He didn't go into detail, but I got the impression that she comforted him for what he tried to do and probably he lives in fear of Ti and Jasper."

"Do you think they have attacked him?" Nick asked.

"I doubt so recently, but they have had decades to bully and threaten him," Cal said.

"Okay, let's keep someone on Mr. Moreau to keep him safe. We have something to discuss this evening after everyone gets dinner. It's about seven now, so let's meet back here at ten-thirty. Phil, before you take off for dinner would you ask Sinclair to come up?"

"Sure," Phil said, "but you had better be prepared. He is not happy with you at all. So if I were you, I would take care of the case business first."

Nick sighed. "Okay, ask him if he has time to come up."

Chapter 35

Nick sat at the conference table as Sinclair sauntered into the room, carrying a paper bag. He wasn't smiling.

"What did you fuck up today, Mr. Caldwell?" Sinclair asked.

Nick replied, "The usual, why do you ask? You have an interest in this case?"

"Do I have an interest in this case," Sinclair said.

"Yeah, do you have an interest in this case?" Nick asked.

Sinclair gave him the look, one that was usually followed by a punch or in extreme cases someone getting shot.

"Because all I have heard since you called me about this is you whining and yelling at everyone but not coming up with any solutions or suggestions," Nick said.

"Go to hell," Sinclair said.

"I will one day, but since you will probably get there before me, could you save me a seat in the cafeteria?" Nick asked.

Nick thought he saw Sinclair almost smile.

"What do you want, smart ass?" Sinclair said.

"I want you to start carrying your weight and maybe try to sober up every once in a while," Nick said.

"First, I need you to answer a question," Sinclair said.

"What question?" Nick asked.

"That dream I had of you and my daughter, was it real?" the old man said.

Nick was quiet for a moment, then answered, "Yes, and I think she was going to hit on me."

Sinclair actually smiled. "It may have been real, but I know her mother would never let her get within a mile of an asshole detective like you."

"You mean like her mother did?" Nick said, with a smile.

Sinclair laughed. "Good point but at least her mother married a handsome, debonaire and distinguished detective," he said. "What do you need me to do?"

"What I don't need is you shooting any of the Barbeaus," Nick said.

"I can hold off from doing that for a while," Sinclair said.

"Good," Nick said, "do you still have any friends in the New Orleans Police Department?"

"Why do you ask?" Sinclair asked.

"Because it is time to bring them into this," Nick said. "I think soon we're going to break the case and we are going to want their cooperation and they should have the collar on this."

"You mean the same deal we had in Chicago with the Crowe case and in St. Louis with that cold case?" Sinclair asked.

"Exactly like that," Nick said. "We are all set technically; Greg has that place wired for sound and pictures. If we get something that could lead to a conviction, we need the police involved."

"Is Fontane responsible?" Sinclair asked.

"No, not the old man, but we think Ti may be," Nick said.

"The kid?" Sinclair asked.

"Maybe, but whoever is responsible keeps souvenirs," Nick said.

"Where did you get that information?" Sinclair asked.

"A confidential source," Nick said.

"Will they testify at trial?" Sinclair asked.

Nick looked at him and said, "No, but if they did, it would be worth seeing."

Sinclair smiled sadly, and looked down.

"Do you think the old man is protecting the kid?" Sinclair asked

"No, no I don't. I think he sees that Ti is an asshole, but I don't think he would believe that his son is capable of anything like this," Nick said. "I also think that it is getting close to the time when we have to let him know who we are. That is another reason we need the police involved, in case anyone tries to run. Can you set up a meeting away from the police offices?"

"I can," Sinclair said. "The current chief is the son of one of my partners when I was in the department. His dad, who ended up a Deputy Chief worked on this case, and the current chief was a young uniform cop who was also on the case. I think we might be able to persuade them. Both of them have the reputation of being good cops with the ability to be flexible. Flexibility is an important quality to have in the department."

"Then let's do it soon," Nick said. "What kind of man is Fontane?"

"What do you mean?" Sinclair asked?

"How do you think he will react when he finds out we been investigating the studio and we are looking for those responsible for the murders and disappearances?" Nick asked.

"Do you like it when people take advantage of you and lie to you?" Sinclair asked.

"I have always figured it was part of the job," Nick said.

They both laughed.

"He will feel betrayed, but you did find out that his studio has ghosts. He has always been obsessed with that," Sinclair said. "Do you think he sincerely wants the people who hurt his dancers to be found and punished."

"I think he does," Nick responded.

"Then explain to him why it was necessary to investigate it the way you have. When we were friends, I always thought he was a fair man. Would you want me there?" Sinclair asked.

"Depends," Nick said. "Are you going to shoot him or Ti?"

Sinclair smiled and said, "No."

"Are you going to shoot me?"

Sinclair smiled again. "Can I think about that and get back to you?"

"Why not," Nick said.

"I have a bone to pick with you," Sinclair said.

"When do you not have a bone to pick with me?" Nick replied.

Sinclair ignored the comment and asked, "After the trouble I went to arranging a quiet romantic dinner for you and Casey, why didn't you follow through, dumb ass?"

"I've been a little busy here, and Casey has been a little busy," Nick said.

"That's bullshit," Sinclair said. "I think I have the answer for you now about whether I am going to shoot you."

Nick ignored his reply. "We're meeting back here later. I'd like you to be at the meeting."

"Fine," Sinclair stood up and tossed the paper back on the table.

"What's this?" Nick asked.

"I got something for you, Idiot," Sinclair said. "Open it."

Nick opened it, it was a novel by Heather Graham.

Sinclair said, "Read it. She writes murder mysteries about detectives who talk to spirits. And her detectives have intimate relationships."

"With ghosts?" Nick said, with a smile.

Sinclair said, "No, jerk, with women…get it?" He turned and walked toward the door and said, "See you at the meeting later. I have to go clean my gun."

Nick smiled and said to himself, "The old man is back." Then he picked up the book and opened it to Chapter One.

Chapter 36

I have asked Sinclair to be here tonight," Nick began, "and I have asked him to take a more active role in the investigation now that we are at a point to start bringing it together. I want to discuss how we proceed from here.... Bart."

"Okay, at this point we have identified seven likely victims and we believe there are probably more. Casey and Phil are still digging," Bart said. "From the information we have we are guessing that there is a pattern of one victim every one to three years."

Cal asked, "How did you come up with that number pattern?"

"Felix, Greg and I looked at the seven we have confirmed and in two cases we have either a gap between the killings and the disappearances. With a sample this small we are only guessing," Bart said.

"What significance does this have?" Alana asked.

Greg said, "We have discussed a couple theories. The first is that this is not a serial killer without some control. The second is that this perp is patient and that he chooses his victims carefully and possibly tries to cultivate a type of relationship with them."

"Also, we believe that if at some point of the relationship dance, they don't get what they want, they will take what they want and dispose of the victim in some way, so they are not discovered," Felix said. "The victims that have been discovered were not just murdered but beaten before they were murdered."

Bart continued, "This person or persons obviously have a lot of rage. They probably can control most of their rage within bounds coming off as emotional hot heads or they are maybe able to hide it in some other way."

"You said person or persons," Constance said. "Do you believe there is more than one person doing this?"

Bart replied, "We are beginning to believe that there may be at least one other, maybe two, because we believe that they were assaulted and murdered at the studio and transported somewhere else."

"We also are thinking maybe there is a third," Nick said.

"A third?" Bob asked.

"Yes, we have discussed there could be a third that is not involved with the murders but keeps a cool head and covers up afterwards to protect the murders and the reputation of the studio," Nick said. "This could be someone that would not be suspected."

"Where do we go from here?" Bob asked.

"We keep investigating if there are other victims and the studio staff. And Sinclair is going to set up a meeting with the New Orleans P.D." Nick said. "It's time to bring them in, the way we did in St. Louis and with my brother Wil and the Chicago P.D. in the Crowe case. I think we may need them to get warrants."

Phil asked, "Same deal, we build the case, and they get the collar, but we are still involved after we invite them in?"

"Yep," Nick said.

"So, we will be consultants to the police department, and they have invited us to come in to do an undercover operation?" Phil asked.

"You know the dance, Phil," Nick said.

"How do we explain a Chicago-based agency was brought in?" Phil asked.

"Mr. Sinclair arranged it with the New Orleans Chief to bring us in to find the truth about his daughter, and he is our client of record, "Nick said.

"Works for me," Phil said.

"Nick, do I need to work on getting the paperwork together?" Casey asked.

"Yeah, we'll need a letter from Sinclair requesting us and a letter of notification that we accept their invitation to go undercover for investigative purposes. Also, could you do the letters from the cops to us, just put a package together that if any press starts snooping around everyone is covered," Nick said.

"Sometimes I feel like we work for the 'Outfit'," Phil said, with a grin.

"Don't worry, I'm pretty sure Nick can get them down here if we need them," Sinclair said, with a smile.

"Yeah," Bob said, "I can call Laura and have her ask the twins to call their Uncle Antonio."

"You know, Nick, it might not be a bad idea to call Joey and find out if he has any friends down here to make sure no one leaves town in a hurry," Phil said.

Nick looked at his brother. "I don't think we need to do that...just yet."

"Yeah, they're pretty good at difficult interrogations too," Bart said, with a laugh.

"May we get back to business?" Nick said.

"Whatever you say, Don Caldwell...I mean, Daddy," Katie said, laughing.

"Are you all done?" Nick asked. "Why don't we all take a break."

+

A few years ago, Nick had solved the murder of the uncle of a retired Chicago mob boss, Joey "the Bat" Carrandini. They ended up becoming friends, and Joey's brother Anthony had appointed himself as protector of the Caldwell family, particularly Nick's sister, Laura, and his brother-in -law, Bob, and their twins. Only in Chicago would this be possible or plausible. Since then, Nick's staff has been merciless with the Godfather jokes.

+

Bart gathered the group back together.

Nick sat at the table and read a file until they were all assembled.

"Now where were we before you pissed me off?" Nick said. "We need to focus here. I am not going to keep you much longer this evening. Bart, Greg, and I are going back to the studio this evening."

"We have a beginning of a plan," Bart said. "Our objective when we started was to identify and find the parties responsible for Deidra Stewart's death. We think we have narrowed the possibilities."

"We believe that those responsible for Deidra's death are also involved in a series of murders and disappearances that are connected with the Barbeau Studio," Nick added. "We believe that the founder is not part of this, or at least we have not found any direct or indirect evidence that he is involved. We have identified two suspects and are keeping an open mind that there may be more. We have a source that believes that the person or persons responsible may be collectors and that somewhere in the building there may be a souvenir box or chest. Casey has confirmed with the families of the deceased women that something that was important to each of the victims was missing. In the case of Deidra, it was a silver locket with her initials on it and pictures of her mother and her father in it."

Sinclair sat showing no emotion.

Nick continued, "As I said, we think it is in the building. The most logical places to look would be on the fifth floor, basement and sub-basement, but there has been so much construction and restoration in the building it could be anywhere, and we are on the clock."

"Casey, would you and Phil go through all the building plans that have been filed from 1990 to the present. Compare them and see if there is anything that is different from the most current plan," Bart said. "Greg, Cal, and Felix, would you work with Casey and Phil and then we would like you to look at floors one through four and look to see if there have been any alterations that don't match the plans. Look for walls and floors in the office areas and rehearsal spaces and check out the performance auditorium. They have several floor configurations for dance floors."

"Bart, this is going to take some time to do all this," Felix said.

"It will," Bart said, "but we have to find where this box is hidden."

"Greg, I know you have installed a lot of cameras already, but call Chicago and have them send additional cameras and audio equipment. I don't want any blind spots on the fifth floor and basements," Nick said.

"When are we going to do all this?" Greg asked.

"We're going to have to do most of this at night," Nick said. "Bart has already arranged to have our van driven down here tomorrow. Make your call after we finish and have them bring the cameras and any other equipment you need loaded in the van."

"You know we are violating several laws," Felix said.

"Don't worry about that," Sinclair said. "We will meet with the police tomorrow, and we will have the warrants we will need and dated properly to ensure our collective asses are covered."

"How's that going to work?" Felix asked.

Sinclair smiled. "Felix, this is New Orleans, this is a magical place."

"Okay, that's it for tonight," Nick said. "Greg, make the call. Bart and I will wait in the car. Everybody should be out of the studio by now."

Chapter 37

Nick opened the front door of the studio with the key that Fontane had given them. The lobby was dark as they headed for the stairway that led up to the fifth floor.

"Nick," Bart said.

"What?" Nick said.

Greg said, "The reception desk."

"What about it?" Nick said.

"Just look, dammit," Bart said.

Nick turned and saw a young woman at the desk. She motioned them to her. They had never seen her before. The woman was in her late teens with long raven colored hair and piercing blue eyes.

"Mr. Caldwell?" she said.

"Yes," Nick said.

"I have a message for you and your associates," she said.

"A message?" Nick asked.

"Yes, a message," she said.

"From whom?" Nick asked.

"From your new friend," she said. "She told me to tell you that my name is Kayla Shaw."

"Is that the message?" Nick asked.

"Not all of it," Kayla said.

"What's the rest of it?" Nick asked.

"Mr. Caldwell, I am number eleven and I am not the last," Kayla said. "I wore an emerald ring my grandmother gave me. They took it."

"You want me to find your ring?" Nick asked.

"Yes, and I want you to find me, so I can be at peace," she said.

Then she was gone.

They looked at each other.

"Call Phil right now," Nick said. "Have him run a check on a Kayla Shaw."

Greg called Phil and relayed the information. "He'll call us back."

They went to the fifth floor. Nick sat on the old couch across from Bart. Greg began checking the cameras they had in place.

"You know Deidra sent her to you," Bart said.

Nick said nothing.

"She is number eleven and not the last," Bart said. "She told us what souvenir they took from her."

Nick's phone buzzed. "What did you find?"

Phil replied, "Kayla Dianne Shaw, nineteen years old, born in Natchez, Mississippi, moved to New Orleans for high school. Attended New Orleans Center for Creative Arts."

"Do you have a picture?" Nick asked.

"Yes," Phil said, "she is Caucasian, looks like she has dark hair."

"Anything else?" Nick asked.

"Nick, she went missing thirteen years ago on her way home from a rehearsal. She apparently stopped to get something at a restaurant, had coffee, and was never seen again. I don't think I have to tell you where she was rehearsing," Phil said.

"Keep looking," Nick said.

"Do you think she is number eight?" Phil asked.

"No, she is number eleven," Nick said.

"Oh, my God," Phil said. "How did you find out about her?"

"She was waiting for us when we arrived. She told us she wanted us to find her ring that her grandmother gave her," Nick said. "Then she asked us to find her so that she can be at peace."

Phil was quiet for a moment, "Okay, Casey and I will see what else we can find. See you later."

+

Greg went to the basements and started to check the surveillance cameras that he had already placed there a few days ago, and he was looking for additional locations for cameras. He planned to do this on all the floors. When he finished, he wanted to make sure that if the box of souvenirs were in the building and if someone would try to retrieve it, they would see them and hopefully be able to identify them.

Nick and Bart went to the fifth floor.

"You okay," Bart asked.

"Hell no, I'm not okay. Eleven? How many more, Bart? How many more of these women have these sons of bitches killed? How many families have they destroyed? How many mother's and fathers' hearts have they broken? It ends with us this time, one way or another, it ends with us," Nick said.

"We will stop it, Nick, we're close," Bart said.

"Not close enough. Maybe I should just tell Sinclair to come down here and end these assholes," Nick said.

"Then what, visit Sinclair at Angola and bring him a cake with a file in it each month?" Bart said.

"How do you figure we're close?" Nick said.

"What is it you say," Bart said, "facts and evidence. We have someone who will testify that Ti and this Jasper idiot abused these women, forced them to comply with their whims. We have spirits who are trying to help us find the truth, we know that the perp or perps keep souvenirs and tomorrow you and Sinclair are going to get the police involved and then we can get them to issue warrants."

"There is something that still bothers me about all this, and I don't know what it is yet," Nick said. "I can't put my finger on it, but we're missing something obvious. Deidra said, 'dig deeper.' We have two good suspects but there is something wrong here. Do you really believe that Ti and Jasper are smart enough to pull this off for this long?"

"If there was anyone else, they wouldn't be my first choice," Bart said, "but they had motive, they didn't want the girls to reveal what they were doing. They had opportunity, they were around them all the time. And they had the means and a place where they would not be disturbed and a way to transport them. Are you saying there is someone else involved?"

"I'm saying, I don't know. I agree that they are involved, but I still feel we are missing something," Nick said. "We need to look at this a different way and I don't know what that way is."

"Yet, we don't know what that way is...yet," Bart said, "but we will."

"This is like the old days, isn't it?" Nick said.

"You mean when we didn't know jack and we didn't have any money and the first of the month was always an adventure?" Bart said.

"Yeah, when it was just you, me, Felix, Nan, and Mrs. Marbles? When we all worked out of the offices above Blackie's, and we were lucky to get enough clients to pay the rent and the phone bill."

"Don't forget Duke the Wonder Dog. After all, he took a bullet for you and saved your life," Bart said.

"I will never forget Duke and I will never forget his sister," Nick said.

"Tina, the old girl went too early," Bart said. "I remember that she would lie on the couch in the old conference room and look out the window. She always looked so sad. I also remember when you got Baron and all he did when he was a puppy was to follow Duke around like he was in an apprentice program."

"I miss Nan, too; she was our first new hire," Nick said. "I think she still believes the only reason we brought her on was because her name was Nancy Drew. I admit I liked the idea of having Nancy Drew on staff, just to see the clients face when she introduced herself. Now she is Special Agent Nancy Drew, F.B.I."

"I'm happy for her," Bart said.

"I'm proud of her," Nick said.

"So, answer my question," Nick said. "Do you miss those days when you are sitting in that posh executive office?"

144

"That wasn't your question. Your question was, this is like the old days, isn't it? The answer to that question is, yes, this case is like the old days, only we eat better when we travel now. The answer to the question, 'do I miss it,' the answer to that question is every damned day. I miss most of all when we all would close the office and go down to Blackie's and hang out after work or when we were celebrating closing a case."

"They had great coffee and the chili was great," Nick said.

"That they did," Bart said. "Nick, when this is over, you have to do what's best for you. I don't want you to leave Chicago, but if you need a new start, I'll back whatever you want to do."

"I know," Nick said.

"Jonathon told me that since he is in the Bears front office now, you can sit in the corporate boxes for the Bears games," Bart said.

"Your hubby is a good man," Nick said. "I mean is there that much of a demand for Bears tickets these days?"

"We don't talk about that at home," Bart said, and they both laughed.

"Do you think Greg is about done?" Nick asked

"Done or not let's get him and go," Bart said.

Bart called Greg and asked him to meet them in the lobby. They walked down to the lobby; Greg was waiting by the reception desk. Kayla Shaw was still behind the desk.

Nick walked over and said, "Is there anything else, Kayla?"

"Yes, Mr. Caldwell," she said.

"What is it," Nick said.

"Your friend asked me to tell you, 'It doesn't matter if you dig deeper if you're digging in the wrong place.' That is what she told me to tell you," Kayla said.

"Did Ms. Stewart tell you where the right place is?" Nick asked.

"Yes." she said.

"Okay, where?" Nick asked.

"Where you least suspect it and where you're not looking," Kayla said and faded away.

Nick turned to Bart. "I was wrong. Deidra is not almost as irritating as her father, I think she has surpassed him."

As they pushed the door open, they heard a stack of brochures hit the floor.

"Goodnight, Deidra," Nick said, walking out.

Chapter 38

Whenever Nick entered a police department headquarters it brought back memories, bad memories. He was an officer in the Chicago Police Department and eventually became a detective. His grandfathers were cops; his father was a cop; his brother was a cop; so, he became a cop. He always wondered why rising through the ranks, the higher you rose the bigger jerk you became on the job. At least that how it seemed in Chicago. The rank and file guys were good folks, but the ambitious ones, well the more stripes and hardware they got, the bigger jerks they became.

He got disenchanted with his department when it took years to solve the murder of his daughter and unborn child who were cut down in a drive-by shooting. The case wasn't solved until help was provided by his detective agency and the assistance of Sinclair Stewart and a certain retired wise guy named Joey 'The Bat' Carrandini.

After his children's death he lost everything. He not only lost his children, he lost his wife, he lost interest in his job, and he lost interest in everything but his two dogs, Duke and Tina. He quit the force, and with the help of a friend from Loyola who was beginning a career as a shrink he was gradually able to move forward. That is when he went back to school and got three degrees, one of them was in law. He passed the Bar but never practiced, and when asked why, he would say that he had too much respect for himself. When he was asked why he got three degrees, he would say that it took him that long to get good seats at the football games and besides he liked Ann Arbor. He liked the campus and the classes, and he particularly liked the Cottage Inn pizza.

With his law degree and other graduate degrees, he moved back to Chicago. One happy hour he was having several drinks with his shrink friend at Blackie's, a former speakeasy during prohibition. He convinced his friend that it would be great for the two of them to start a private investigation agency. His friend agreed and they immediately rushed to Marshalls in the loop and bought two trench coats. The next day they met for lunch at Blackie's and still thought it was a good idea. So, they talked to Jeff, the owner of Blackie's and convinced him that it would be a great idea for him to rent them an office over the bar. Now that they had an office and two very cool trench coats they realized something was missing. They were pondering this question when Jeff came by with a pot of coffee. They told him they thought something was missing or that they had forgotten something. Jeff poured them coffee and said, "Maybe you should leave here a few hours a day and try to find some clients, so you can pay the rent for your new office?"

So, they did, and since that evening Bart and Nick were best friends and business partners. It was the first time since losing his family that Nick felt he had a reason to move forward with his life. He liked being a Private I. He liked working cases...he really liked his trench coat.

This morning he didn't like going to the NOLA PD office of administration.

Sinclair and Nick were shown to the Deputy Chief's office. Standing to greet them was Theodore Robert Bryant, Jr., he held out his hand to Sinclair. Theodore Robert Bryant Jr. could have played defensive end for the Saints or been a stunt double for Woody Strode, an actor that was a regular in John Wayne films.

"How's your dad," Sinclair said.

"He's good, Sinclair. I didn't get a chance to thank you at Mom's funeral."

"No need, she was a fine woman," Sinclair said. "How is everyone else?"

"Dad's still a little low," Robert said.

"I'll call him today," Sinclair said. "This is Nick Caldwell."

"I've heard a lot about you," Robert said.

"I hope some of it was good," Nick replied.

"I know your brother, Wil," Robert said.

"Too bad, I was hoping to make a good impression," Nick said.

"No, your brother is very proud of you," Robert said.

"He doesn't seem proud of me when he speaks to me," Nick said.

Robert laughed. "Come on, he's your big brother, cut him some slack."

"Did you read the file I sent?" Sinclair asked.

"Yes, you know that you and your crew have bent a lot of rules and a few laws. So many in fact, I was thinking about talking to the chief to see if we could offer you a job." Robert laughed. "Seriously, you did good work so far, but we're going to have to clean up some things."

"We understand," Nick said.

"Here's what we need. We have drafted a letter of agreement inviting Caldwell and Cheswick Investigations to help our department work on cleaning up some cold cases," Robert said, "authorizing you to do undercover investigations for the purpose of investigating some unsolved murders, missing persons, and other cold cases. After your work on the Crowe case and the case up the river in St. Louis, it was an easy sell. We will provide any resources you need."

"Thank you," Nick said. "We would like your department to handle any evidence we get to protect the chain of custody," Nick said. "We are going to want to have you in on all the video surveillance, including all the interview audios."

"You will have the proper warrants for that by this afternoon and I have taken the liberty of assigning a liaison from our department," Robert said.

"Good, the more the merrier," Nick said. "Get us the name and send him over."

"I'm sending Sergeant Lucas Bryant," Robert said.

"Little Luke is a Sergeant?" Sinclair said, smiling.

"Yep, so if he doesn't do a good job, I can tattle on him to Dad, and little Luke is grown up to be about 6'6," Robert said, with a laugh.

"The other thing that I want to be clear about is we will testify if needed, but it's your show. You tell us when we get enough for you to take it to your prosecutor. We don't want publicity or credit. Our effort is self-funded. While and after we're done working the case from this point on, it's all yours," Nick said.

"I have a request to make," Robert said. "Sinclair, you know Dad worked this case until he retired and continued to work it after he retired. He got his PI card. Would it be okay with you if he observed?"

"Observed?" Nick said. "Hell yes, we could use someone who knows this case."

"Tell that old man that he should get his butt over to my house, that's where we're set up," Sinclair said. "When we break this, he and I can stand together when you make the arrests."

"When we break this, I think your dad and Sinclair should cuff them," Nick said, "and add his name on the letter of agreement."

Robert smiled. "Thank you."

"I'll have Felix and Greg call your tech guys about the audio and video feeds," Nick said.

"We should have everything in place by early afternoon," Robert said.

As Nick and Sinclair walked out of the department, Nick said, "That was easy."

Sinclair smiled. "That's the reason we call NOLA, the Big Easy...well, that's one of the reasons."

Chapter 39

When they returned to Sinclair's, Nick gathered everyone in in the ballroom.

"We have the cooperation of the New Orleans Police Department, thanks to the cranky old gentleman sitting at the end of the table," Nick said.

Sinclair stood, took a bow and then flipped Nick off to the delight of the staff. Baron and Ruby were sitting next to Sinclair and barked their approval.

"Chief Bryant has assigned Sergeant Lucas Bryant as the department's liaison with us, and we will cooperate fully with him. Everyone get all the information that you have acquired through the investigation and get it to Casey and Phil and help them get it copied and boxed.

Greg and Felix, can we get copies of all the surveillance videos and audio for them as well. Also, when Lucas gets here speak to him about how we can get them on our live-feed surveillance. Also, ask him if they can spare a few folks to watch the feed. Greg, are the other cameras here yet?"

"They arrived this morning," Greg said.

"Can we get them all in place tonight?" Nick asked.

Greg looked at Felix and he nodded. "We can, all we really have left are the offices."

"Great," Nick said, "Katie and Cal, I want everyone interviewed again, this time Cal you interview the women and Katie the men. This time push a little."

"Bob and Constance, can you run a full background on the folks they are interviewing?"

"Alana, work with Phil and Casey. Cal and Katie, exchange your notes with each other, find the hot spots."

"Are we still looking at Ti and Jasper as suspects?" Cal asked.

"We are, but I mentioned to you that I thought we were missing something," Nick said.

"What will you be doing?" Katie asked.

"Bart, Sinclair and I will be working with T.R. Bryant Sr., Chief Bryant's father and Sinclair's partner when he was with NOLA PD," Nick said. "No one knows as much about this case as Sinclair and Mr. Bryant. We expect Mr. Bryant Sr. to join us this evening and Lucas will be here sometime this afternoon."

There was a knock on the Ballroom door. "Come in," Nick said.

Lucas Bryant entered the room; he could have been the Chief's twin only ten years younger.

Sinclair said," Welcome, Luke."

Luke walked over and he smiled and said, "Good to see you, Uncle Sin."

Phil said, "You got that right."

"Are you lookin' to get shot, sonny," Sinclair said.

"No sir," Phil said, "but I never get tired of you threatening me."

Nick introduced Lucas around and brought him up to speed about what was going on.

"What can I do to help," Lucas asked.

"Probably the best thing to do is as we get the information together that we have already collected why don't you start looking at it," Nick said. "You can work with Casey and Phil and when you want to get into the video and audio, Greg will be able to help you. He needs to talk to you about the live feed."

"That reminds me," Lucas said. He opened his briefcase and pulled out a stack of papers. "Here is the letter from the department authorizing Caldwell & Cheswick to assist in the cold cases assigned to you by the New Orleans Police Department. Here is a letter stating that we have deputized you to conduct an investigation with us and here is a stack of warrants when and if we need them."

"So, all we will need to do is fill them out and you will get them to a judge?" Nick asked.

Lucas smiled. "All you have to do is fill them out; the judge has already signed them."

"How did your brother get a judge to sign off on these warrants?" Nick asked.

"He has an interest in what you are doing and wants to help in any way he can," Lucas said.

"An interest in these cases?"

"Yes," Lucas said, "Judge Shaw's granddaughter went missing a few years ago. It destroyed his son and daughter-in-law because they never knew what happened and they were afraid that she was dead, and they never were able to give her a proper funeral."

Knowing the answer to his question, Nick asked, "What was his granddaughter's name?"

"Kayla, Kayla Dianne Shaw," Lucas said.

Nick looked at Bart and Greg, and said, "We have run across that name in our investigation as a possible victim."

"It really caused some problems with the family. Her father and mother said that they had seen her spirit around the quarter and at their home. They for years would go to spiritualists trying to contact her," Lucas said. "There was a rumor that the Judge thought he saw her near the St. Louis Cathedral one Sunday, but then he said he missed her so much and wanted to see her so badly that his mind was playing tricks on him."

"What do you think?" Nick asked.

"Mr. Caldwell, I am a police officer and I have to deal with facts and evidence," Lucas said.

"I understand," Nick said.

"But this is New Orleans and in New Orleans I believe anything could happen. It is a beautiful place, but it is also a mystical place and sometimes it's just a damned weird place. So, as a lifelong resident, I tend to lean to anything could happen here."

"I'm leaning that way myself," Nick said.

Chapter 40

Nick walked into the Ballroom to check on the progress. The material for the police was being gathered, copied and boxed. The plan was to get it to Chief Bryant in the morning.

"How's it going?" Nick asked.

"Very well," Casey said, "we'll have it on its way by midnight."

"If we get it to them by ten in the morning that will be fine," Nick said.

"Give everyone a dinner break and do you have the company card, still?" he asked.

"Yes," she said, "why?"

"Take everyone out somewhere on us," Nick said.

"That's about ten people," she said.

"Yeah, money is no object...for Bart." He laughed. "And once we get this thing wrapped up, I think I owe you a dinner," Nick said. "I was thinking, do they have a nice McDonalds near here?"

Casey smiled. "You think you're funny, but you're not."

"You think I haven't heard that before?" Nick said.

"Oh no, I know you hear that all the time," Casey said, with a laugh.

"Okay, okay, do they have Denny's down here?" Nick said.

"Why don't you go somewhere," she said.

"Where?" Nick said.

"Anywhere," she said, "as long as it's not here. Oh, are you, Bart and Sinclair going that would make it thirteen?"

"Thirteen is unlucky, no we're staying here and will wait for T. R. to get here," Nick said. "Sinclair thinks we should sit down with him and go over his investigations."

"I thought he was coming over earlier" she said.

"He was, but he decided to have all his case files sent over and he wanted to look at a few of the files before he sent them over," Nick said.

"How close do you think we are to getting this thing solved?" she asked.

"I will have a better idea after we meet T.R.," Nick said. "There is something we are missing."

"You think there are others involved, don't you?" Casey said.

"I think it is a possibility and I have an idea who it might be," Nick said.

"I've been going over the interviews again, and I have an idea who else might be involved. I looked at the interviews of the other employees, too, that were done initially," she said.

She walked over to her desk and showed Nick a file. The file had background material and comments from first interviews that covered some casual gossip from the employees with less tenure than the nine that were interviewed by Cal and Katie. Casey had highlighted a few names of those she thought might be involved.

"What do you think?" she said.

"I think," Nick said, "great minds think alike, but we're going to need more. Have you shared this with anyone?"

"No, I wanted you to see this first," she said.

"Maybe I will owe you two dinners at Denny's," Nick said.

Phil walked up to them, "T.R.'s files arrived. We loaded them into the dining room."

"Good, I'll be down in a minute," Nick said. "Phil, get everyone together, we're springing for dinner out. Make sure everyone is back in a couple of hours. Take the vans."

Chapter 41

All the Bryant's were impressive but T.R. was impressive and distinguished. He carried himself like a general who had waged countless campaigns against the enemies of the people of New Orleans. In the old days, he would have been called a peace officer. It was obvious why he and Sinclair were friends and partners. He had continued to work on this case even when leads went cold; he continued to work on it after he retired. He worked on it because Deidra called him 'Uncle T.R.' Every cop has a case that got to them, the one that was always in the back of their minds, the one that they hadn't solved...yet. The criminals who got away. The case that would haunt them until it was solved, or they went to the grave. For T.R. this was about family.

"Nick, may I present my friend, T.R. Bryant," Sinclair said.

"Mr. Bryant, it is an honor," Nick said.

"Nice to meet you," T.R. said. "May I ask you a question?"

"Certainly," Nick said.

"Is Sinclair as big a pain in the ass to work with as he was when I worked with him?"

"Sir, I understand you haven't worked with him in several years," Nick said.

"That's correct," T.R. said.

"Then as you can imagine, he has used those years to perfect being a classic pain in the ass," Nick said.

T.R. laughed and turned to Sinclair and said, "I like him."

"That's good, not many do," Sinclair replied.

"Does he still threaten to shoot people?" T.R. asked.

"Always," Nick said.

"May I suggest we adjourn to the dining room, pour some whiskey, and talk about how to catch these assholes," Sinclair said, "so I get the opportunity to shoot them?"

Bart was waiting for them in the dining room looking at the twenty-five to thirty boxes that were stacked against one of the walls.

Sinclair introduced Bart as the brains of Caldwell and Cheswick Investigations.

They sat at the large table and Sinclair poured them all a drink.

Baron sat on the floor between Nick and Sinclair and Ruby decided that T.R. was her new best friend. She sat close to him so he could scratch her ears and he did.

They all exchanged war stories during dinner. T.R. said that he loved reading the books about Nick's cases, obviously primed to say that by Sinclair.

Nick blushed and said, "They're fiction."

Sinclair laughed and said, "Obviously."

"I figured that out because Sinclair sounds smart in the books," T.R. teased.

After dinner they settled into Sinclair's study.

"How to you think I could assist you in your investigation?" T.R. asked.

"No one knows this case better than you and Sinclair," Nick said. "I would like you to look at what we have gathered to see if you see any patterns or if you notice anything that we should pursue. I know that you have interviewed everyone connected with the Studio."

T.R. said "That's correct."

"What was your impression of them?" Nick asked.

"Could you tell me what your theory is about the case?"

"Happy to," Bart said, "We are leaning to it being an inside job. That the disappearances and deaths are somehow connected to the Studio."

"We don't think Fontaine is involved," Nick said, "but if we had a suspect list Ti and Jasper would be on it. I am beginning to think that there may be others."

"Why have you cleared Fontaine?" T.R. asked.

157

"We don't see him as a doer," Bart said, "but we haven't ruled him out as knowing something. Maybe he is protecting Ti or the Studio."

"I have always thought that the most he could be guilty of was looking the other way. He may suspect something, but he is in denial," T.R. said. "But that kid of his is a piece of work. I don't think he is a killer, but he is hostile all the time. He has been waiting for the old man to retire and Fontaine doesn't seem to be going anywhere until his grandson is ready to take over. As for Jasper, he is a letch and an idiot. I do believe, like you, that they are involved in some way. You say that you have interviewed all the senior members of the staff?"

"Yes," Bart said.

"It sounds like you focused on Ti and Jasper," T.R. said. "The one thing I am convinced about is that whole group of senior employees came on staff believing that Ti would take over. None of them are loyal to the old man except his grandson Trip. Also, we found that senior group a collection of creeps in some way or another. The killer could be in that group, but some of them have some real creeps as associates. Moore the set designer and the stage manager, what's his name?"

"Santos," Nick said.

"There were rumors that they would let some real creeps hang around to watch the dancers warm up and rehearse. It got so bad that the old man found out and ran them off and threatened to fire Moore and Santos. Ti stepped in and saved their jobs," T.R. continued.

"You probably heard about Ti and Ava Johnson. She and Ti had a thing. That's why Trip's mom left him. The last we heard, Ti broke it off, but Ava is available to him any time. She still has hope."

"We also investigated rumors that some of the dancers were sexually abused, but we could never get anyone to come forward and we couldn't get any proof and members of the staff never confirmed it."

"Where did you hear about the abuse?" Nick asked.

"From that real squirrelly little guy, Moreau, but he has a real grudge against Ti and Jasper because they torment him like they all were in high school," T.R. said. "Moreau is very strange even by New Orleans standards. We always thought he knew more than he told us but was afraid of what would happen to him if he said more. But he seemed sincerely protective of the dancers. Is any of this helpful?"

"Very," Nick said. "We suspected that there was history between Ava and Ti, but we didn't know that it was that extensive. We also didn't know that Moore and Santos were letting unauthorized folks into the Studio."

"I will help you all I can, but I have only one request," T.R. said.

"What's that?" Nick asked.

"When this goes down, promise me, when you have enough to make an arrest, I would like to be there standing next to this man," T.R. pointed to Sinclair, "when you cuff the bastard or bastards responsible for this."

"I promise," Nick said. "May I ask one more question?"

"Sure," T.R. said.

"How many women do you believe are possible victims in this case?" Nick asked.

T.R. thought for a minute. "Including murder victims we know about and missing persons we believe to be connected to the Studio in some way? If I had to guess," T.R. said, "somewhere between ten and twenty-five, maybe more. I base that on the number of victims and a few of the missing persons that had some connection with the studio. I have more detailed information in the files about this that we never released. How many do you think there have been?"

"I know for sure at least eleven," Nick said.

Nick, Bart and Sinclair looked at each other.

Bart said, "Oh, my God."

Sinclair said, "God has nothing to do with this."

Chapter 42

Casey took the staff to Pat O'Brien's and apparently she put a one drink maximum into effect because there was still a lot of work to do that night.

The chief had sent six officers to Sinclair's to monitor the video feed from the studio and to help go through the files and help Casey match them up with the information that had been gathered by the Chicago group.

When they got back, Nick and Bart got Greg, loaded up the equipment and headed to the Studio.

"Where do you want me to put the cameras up tonight? Greg asked.

Do you have all of the offices of the administrators done and the hallways on the administration floor?" Nick asked.

Greg pulled out his list, I have all nine with one camera in each," Greg said.

"Good," Nick said, "I want you to double up on Thompson, Moore, Santos, Marchal, Ti and Moreau."

"Moreau? I thought he was one of the good guys," Greg said.

"As far as we know he is," Nick said, "but something T.R. said got me thinking."

"Have you seen his office?" Greg asked.

"No, why?" Nick said.

"It looks like it could be a side room at the Vatican," Greg said.

"What do you mean?" Nick asked.

"He has a lot of religious artifacts; I haven't seen that many statues in a room since I was at Loyola. He takes his faith seriously," Greg said. "There are statues of saints I hadn't even heard of before."

"Maybe you should have paid more attention in your theology classes at Loyola," Nick said.

"Funny, Pop, I've heard of the big-time saints," Greg said, "like Mary Magdalene and St. Christopher but who is St. Vitas?"

"He is the patron saint of dance," Bart said.

"Okay, but St. Martin de Pores or St. Agnes or Rose of Lima, none of them made the greatest hits of saints at Loyola, and who was St. Olga for God's sake?" Greg asked. "He's even got one of those kneelers in there."

"Aren't you glad that we sent him to a prestigious Jesuit university?" Nick said to Bart.

"Worth every penny. He did pronounce the names correctly," Bart replied.

"You both think you're funny, but you're not," Greg said.

"That's the second time I've heard that today," Nick said.

"Listen, all those statues looking at you at night is creepy," Greg said.

"Creepier than Kayla Shaw sitting at the front desk in the lobby?" Nick asked.

"Well, no, but she was kind of cute," Greg said.

"She was dead, Greg, a ghost," Nick said.

"Greg, I don't think ghosts date much," Bart said. "Have you ever gone out with a ghost, Nick?"

"I don't think so," Nick said, "unless you count Maureen."

"She doesn't count," Bart said. "She wanted to make you a ghost."

They all laughed. Maureen was the sister of Charlotte, a woman who killed her husband by setting him up to look like he murdered her. He got the needle and Nick figured out she wasn't dead. Nick tracked her down and she shot him, but he got off a shot too and killed her. For some reason this really pissed off her sister, Maureen, who stalked him for a few years and vowed that one day she would kill Nick. And who knows, maybe one day she will.

"What are you guys going to do while I'm working," Greg asked.

"I'm going to the basement; you have that done, right?" Bart asked.

"Yep, basement, sub-basement, exits from the basements, you name it, we can get video," Greg said.

"I will be on the fifth floor, looking around," Nick said. "When you go to Moreau's office, after you set the cameras, if you want to use the kneeler and pray that we solve this case soon so we can all go home, feel free. A little prayer couldn't hurt you, you know."

"You're just a riot tonight," Greg said. "I'm going to the admin floor."

They walked in the lobby which was empty

Nick called to Greg as he walked to the elevator, "Looks like Kayla is off tonight."

Bart headed for the basement and Nick went to the elevator. He got to fifth floor and started looking at the walls and the floor. He and Bart had done this several times.

"Don't you think that doing the same thing over and over again is the definition of insanity, Nick?" He turned to look behind him and then heard "over here, big boy."

Deidra was sitting on the couch smiling. She was wearing a long flowing white gown. "How do you like my duds?"

"You look very nice. Going to a party?" Nick asked.

"No, don't I remind you of a Greek goddess?" she asked.

"I don't know any Greek goddesses," Nick said.

"You do now, I plan to identify as Diana. I saw a statue of her on a school trip to Washington at the Smithsonian. Of course, I think I could also pass as Aphrodite. What do you think?"

"I think you are keeping me from finding your box," Nick said.

She feigned shock and said, "Don't be base, Nicholas, I thought you were a gentleman."

"What?" Nick said. "No, I didn't mean…"

She burst into laughter. "Just messing with you."

"Well, stop, don't you want me to solve the case? Didn't you say dig deeper?" he said.

"So, what did you think of Kayla?" she asked.

"Really nice girl, now could you stop distracting me."

"It's just my luck, of all the gin joints in the world you had to walk into mine," she said, laughing.

The quote is wrong," Nick said.

"Well, excuse me, I just fell out of a hearse…literally," she said.

"Why are you doing this?" Nick asked.

"I am trying to get you to loosen up, so you stop thinking just logically and start thinking creatively. After all, you are trying to catch a killer who works in a creative field…like dance," she said.

"Why don't you just tell me what you know?" Nick said.

"Because that's not the way it is supposed to work and you know it," she said. Then she paused. "Whoops, forget I said that."

"Are you going to help me or not?" Nick asked.

"I already have. I have given you all you need to solve this case, rhymes with…" she said.

Nick said, "What? What are you talking about?"

"Figure it out," she said. "Speaking of figures, do you like mine?"

"Stop it," Nick said. "You're driving me crazy."

"That's a short drive," she said, laughing.

"What?"

"It's because I'm dead isn't?" she said, pouting.

"Oh, for the love of God," Nick said.

"That's more like it," she said. "You know, Nick, if you weren't so old and if I wasn't so dead, I think we could have something." She giggled.

"Old, if you were still alive, we would be around the same age," he said. "What the hell am I talking about?"

She laughed, then became very serious. "Listen, Nick, I want you to remember this conversation, the answers you are looking for are in our screwball comedy banter. You think about this talk we've had; you dream about this talk. You think about this and make the connections you need to make. There is a method to our madness, there is a method to all madness. Look for the pattern, and Nick, Uncle T.R. was right, but just a little on the high side. You have to do this, some things are a group effort, this is not one of them. Now go get Bart and Greg and go get some rest. My dad is counting on you and all the women here are counting on you, so man up, bucko." She smiled.

"Anything else?" Nick asked.

"Yeah, don't be a jerk and don't you dare take her to Denny's for dinner. Maybe you'll get lucky and have breakfast with her too and there better not be a McMuffin on the menu, get it?. Sweet dreams, big boy."

He was alone again.

Chapter 43

When Nick got back from the studio, he went to the kitchen and made a pot of coffee. When it was finished brewing, he went straight to the ballroom and began writing the conversation he had with Deidra. Nick did not have a photographic memory, but he did have an amazing ability to remember important conversations close to verbatim.

He tried to remember each phrase and each sentence. He started looking for keywords. He looked at the sentence 'You think about this talk we've had; you dream about this talk. You think about this and make the connections you need to make.' Make the connections you need to make. He thought connections to what? A person, a place, a piece of information we have or a piece of information the police have or that is in T.R. or Sinclair's files? "What the hell was she talking about?" Nick said out loud. "I have no idea what I am supposed to connect to."

"What else did she say?" he mumbled. "The answer is in the banter? The whole damned conversation was banter."

The conversation that Nick was in with himself went for three more hours. He was still sitting at the desk in a fog of fatigue and caffeine buzz when Sinclair poked his head in and asked, "Are you planning to stay up all night like a dumb ass or are you going to get some rest?"

"What do you think?" Nick said. "I'm working on something here."

"Well, I know you're a dumb ass, but sometimes you fool me and don't act like one," Sinclair said, with a smile.

"I have to figure this out," Nick said.

"You're not going to figure anything out if you don't get some sleep," Sinclair said.

"I'll be fine," Nick said.

"She's getting to you, isn't she?" Sinclair said.

"What? Who?" Nick replied.

"Really, Nick?" Sinclair said.

"I don't know what you're talking about," Nick barked back.

"She is driving you crazy. She used to do that to me and when I told her she was driving me crazy she would say, 'short drive,' then she'd laugh. Sound familiar, big boy?"

Nick looked at him surprised, "How…"

"Did I know?" Sinclair asked, "because I recognize the frustration. She frustrated me too, and I heard the general laughing about it."

"The general?" Nick said.

"Oh yeah, they were thicker than thieves when she was little and alive," Sinclair said. "The general was her imaginary friend, except we could all see him, but we pretended we didn't see him. I am sure now that they have more in common they still share secrets."

"You know, New Orleans is even too weird for me," Nick said.

"Hell, New Orleans is too weird for everybody; we are just used to it," Sinclair said and laughed.

"Do you have any advice?" Nick asked.

"Yeah," Sinclair said, "go to bed and remember that quote from that midnight movie you like, that was filmed in Savannah?"

"What about it?" Nick asked.

"Well, maybe it is true: 'to understand the living, you have to commune with the dead.'"

"That's your advice?" Nick said.
"No, my advice is go to bed and get some rest. I just brought up the quote to mess with you. Can I ask you something?"

"What?" Nick said.

"Is she all right?" Sinclair asked.

"Yes," Nick said, "she is as irritating as you are; in fact I think she has surpassed you."

Sinclair smiled. "That's my girl. Good night, son."

Baron and Ruby were already in bed when Nick got under the covers.

"You look terrible," Baron said.

"I've seen dead squirrels that looked better," Ruby said.

"Can we all just get to sleep?" Nick muttered.

"Sure," Ruby said. "Sweet dreams, big boy."

Nick sat straight up. "What?"

Chapter 44

B art ran the morning meeting. Nick was in his room still trying to figure out Deidra's *"you have all the clues to solve"* message. Nick asked himself was anything that happened last night real. Did Sinclair actually tell me that the general and Deidra were ghost buddies. Am I finally losing it? After all, for years I've been talking to the dogs, and they answer me."

"Hey, hey , hey, Duke told you and I have told you that we don't really talk to you, it's all in your head," Baron said.

"I don't think you're losing it. I think you just have an overactive imagination," Ruby said.

"Thanks, I feel better already," Nick said.

"Overactive imagination? I don't think so, I think that after all the years he gave Bart crap about seeing ghosts now that he sees them, he is suffering from guilt. He's always been good at guilt; that's what Duke told me when I was a pup."

"I don't understand why he got so upset about the ghosts," Ruby said. "We see them all the time." Do you remember last Christmas when Duke visited?"

"Maybe if he just relaxed and stopped trying to be like Sherlock Holmes and started to think more like Sam Spade or Nick Charles, he'd be able to get back to his roots," Baron said. "And if he does that, he might be able to figure out the message Deidra gave him."

"Do you think you could be quiet so I could think here?" Nick said. "Oh, the hell with it, I'm going to the meeting."

+

Bart was setting the assignments for the day when Nick walked in.

"Sleep well?" Bart asked.

Nick just looked at him.

"Okay," Bart said, we were talking about the interviews, any ideas?"

"Yeah, interview Ti, Thompson, Marchal, and Moreau in their offices. Interview the others in the conference room," Nick said. "Katie, when you interview Moore and Santos, let them know that we know they used to let friends in to gawk at the dancers. Hold off doing the interviews until Bart tells you it's a go. I think now that we have NOLA PD with us, we have to talk about some things about the investigation and we are going to have to move quickly."

"Lucas, could you ask Robert if he has time to come over and talk," Nick said.

"Sure," Lucas said, "when?"

"Later this morning," Nick said.

"I'll call him now," Lucas said.

Nick turned to Sinclair and T.R. and Bart. "I would like you in the meeting."

"We'll be there," Sinclair said.

"Bart?" Nick said.

"I'll be there," he said.

Lucas walked up and said, "He's on his way."

"What's this about? T.R. asked.

"I think it's time we came clean with Fontane," Nick said. "Once we do, it will alert everyone and there may be little or no cooperation."

Chapter 45

Chief Bryant walked through the door at one minute before the hour. Clearly the chief was one of those guys that believed that early was on time and on time was late. Nick brought the chief into Sinclair's office. Sinclair, T.R., and Bart were already there. When they were seated Nick began.

"To update the chief," Nick said, "we're going to do another round of interviews with the primary folks of interest. Then, if we are to move forward it may be time to talk with Fontane and Trip. Now that you are involved, Robert, it may be time to drop the undercover ruse and let them know."

"It could give us a chance to see if Fontane knows anything more than he is saying and we can get a temperature on Trip. He and his father are still suspects," Robert said.

"I would suggest that we give it just a little longer," Sinclair said. "Greg set up all those surveillance cameras. We want to make sure that if that souvenir box is found we are ready to watch the cameras and be ready to move in if anyone goes for the box."

"I agree," T.R. said." Sinclair was telling me about what you did on the Crowe case with that warehouse set up. You could do something like that at the studio, couldn't you?"

"What did you do?" Robert asked.

"We were working with my brother Wil and the Chicago PD," Nick said. "We were able to get inside information and we got some Chicago Police into the warehouse before we were going to meet with the Crowes."

"Is that possible here?" Robert asked.

"It's possible, but we would have to set it up," Bart said.

"Yeah, we have the run of the place and Fontane has let us close sections of the building to check if there were any spirits in the building," Nick said. "We could probably get him to let us close off the basement and fifth floor and we could put a few of your officers in there with some of our people."

"I think T.R. has a good point about letting the undercover operation go a few more days before talking to Fontane," Sinclair said.

"It would give us time to think through placement of officers in the building," Robert said. "How many of my guys would you need?"

"Probably four," Nick said. "We could pair them with four of our folks."

Bart asked, "Who are you thinking about putting with Robert's people?"

"Constance, Bob, and Phil and if anything was going down, we'd have Cal, you and I are there anyway. We'd move Greg and Felix back here," Nick said. "I don't think we're looking at the same situation as we had with Crowes. Here, we just want to be sure no one destroys evidence or slips out. We have someone inside to alert us if anything is going on or looks suspicious."

"We do?" Bart asked.

"We do," Nick said.

"Who and for how long?" Bart asked.

"Since the second day we started at the studio," Nick said, "Alex Hicks."

"Who is he?" Bart asked.

"Not he, Alex is she," Nick said.

"You're going to milk this as long as you can, aren't you?" Bart said.

"Do you remember the snarky young woman at the reception desk?"

"Yeah, madam gatekeeper," Bart said.

"Do you recall who interviewed her?" Nick asked.

"No, and come to think of it I didn't see any notes on her interview," Bart said.

"If you would like to see them, I can get them for you," Nick said.

"Why did you interview her?" Bart asked.

"That is an interesting story," Nick said. "would you like to hear it?"

Bart looked at Nick and just shook his head.

"Okay, I will tell you. The second day we were here, I went down to the reception desk, and I found out that Ms. Hicks is the one who did the calls checking up on our credentials. She found nothing out of the ordinary. However, Ms. Hicks has two hobbies, she likes true crime, and she is a voracious consumer of all things that are mysteries and suspense. She listens to the podcasts, watches movies and TV, reads mysteries, and…"

Bart interrupts, "crime and detective fiction."

"Give the man a cigar," Nick said. "So, I am standing by the desk asking her if she could notify me if our team gets any calls. Then Ms. Hicks says, 'Professor Neff, should I give you Mr. Caldwell's messages as well? It won't be any trouble.' From under the counter, she pulls out a copy of *Uncle Joe is Dead* and a scrapbook of articles about Sinclair, Crowley, and us. She had an exceptional section on the McCarty case.

Of course, I denied it and then she said that she cried when Duke died and asked how Baron and Ruby were, and did I bring them with me.

I told her she was mistaken, and she showed me a picture from the Tribune when we announced the cold case project. There we all were. I couldn't let her blow our cover; I asked her what she planned to do? She replied, nothing. She told me that at one time she wanted to be a dancer and after being hit on, she decided to leave, but Fontane offered her a part-time job working with files and records, so she could pay for school. She attends Loyola-New Orleans. Anybody want to guess what her major is?"

Sinclair said, "Criminal Justice?"

"Give that man a cigar," Nick said.

"I prefer a pipe," Sinclair said.

"The she asked if we needed an operative on the inside?" Nick said. "I said that I would appreciate that and if

172

she heard anything I would like to get a heads up. She said she would do that, and told me not to worry, she wouldn't say a thing to anyone."

"Has she gotten you any information?" the chief asked.

"She sent me digital files and records of the women who disappeared," Nick said. "Casey has looked at them and said they helped fill in some blanks."

"Anything else?" Bart asked.

"Yeah, she wants to be an investigator when she gets out of college, and she asked me...wait for it... if Mr. Wells has a girlfriend. I told her when we finished here, she should ask him herself."

Bart and Sinclair laughed.

"Nick, maybe you should hire this kid," Sinclair said.

"I don't know about that, but if she wants to go the academy, I will give her a kick-ass letter," Nick said.

"I would like to meet her when this is over," the chief said.

Chapter 46

Nick and Bart walked up to the reception desk where they were greeted by Ms. Hicks. "Good morning, Professor Neff and Professor Bartholomew. How are you today?"

"We are excellent, how are you?" Nick said.

"Will you be ghost hunting today? Alex said.

"Dr. Bartholomew will be. I need to see the Maestro," Nick said.

"I believe he is in, and he has no appointments, so you can go up," she said.

"Thank you," Nick said.

Bart and Nick took the stairs. "I am going to make the pitch to him to let us close the basement and fifth floor," Nick said. "Why don't you check on the cameras on the fifth and when Cal gets here have him check the basement."

"Okay, tell him we have found a connection and hot spots of activity and we want to take one more good look," Bart said.

Nick knocked on Fontane's door.

"Come in," Fontane said.

"Good morning, Maestro," Nick said, cheerfully.

"Good morning, what can I help you with?" he said.

"Maestro," Nick began, "I want to thank you for allowing us to do our investigation and inform you that we have almost completed it. We should wrap things up by next week. We want to interview the staff to see if there is anything that they may remember but didn't include in the first interview and I would like to ask you if we could, just for the next two or three days close off the fifth floor and both basements? We would like to install some monitoring equipment to get some final readings."

"I can arrange that," Fontane said. "It's going to be lonely around here when you and your troop leave. I have enjoyed talking to you and Dr. Bartholomew. Have you determined if there are spirits here?"

"We have," Nick said, "and we will explain everything to you when we present our report."

"I look forward to it," Fontane said.

+

Cal sat across from Ava Johnson, as they stared at each other.

Ava broke the silence, "You're an attractive man," she said.

"Thank you," he said, "I only have a few questions for you."

"Only a few," she said, "pity."

"We have become concerned some of the spirits here are very restless," he said.

"Really," she said, smirking.

"We believe that several of the women that we encountered were angry," Cal said.

"They're dead. Maybe that's why they are angry," she said.

"We have gotten the feeling that they may be restless because of how they became dead," Cal said.

"I wouldn't know about that," she said.

"It was my understanding that you knew everything that happened in the studio," Cal said.

"What are you implying?" she said.

"Nothing," Cal said, "may I ask you a question?"

"I really must go," she said.

"One question, that's all," Cal said.

She stood to leave.

Cal asked, "With all the years that you have been here and all the young women who have died violently or disappeared, have you ever wondered why or what happened? Did you ever wonder about those women and their connection with this studio?"

Ava glared at him and walked out of the room.

Cal called Nick. "She knows something."

+

Jasper Marchal stood smiling across the table from Katie. "What do you want to talk to me about, sweetheart?"

"Sweetheart? Don't you think I'm a little young for you?" Katie asked.

He laughed.

"I bet you and your buddy Ti like them young. I've seen you looking at all these young dancers," Katie said.

He laughed again. "They're old enough."

"Not old enough to know better," Katie said.

"Are you old enough to know better?" Jasper asked, as he moved towards her.

Katie said, "Hold it there or..."

"Or what?" Jasper asked.

"I am not a naïve eighteen-year-old dancer, and I will kick your nuts up into your throat," Katie said with a smile.

He took a step forward.

"Unless you want your next job to be a soprano in the Vienna Boys Choir, if I were you, I would sit your happy ass down in that chair and answer my questions," Katie said, smiling.

He looked at her and saw something in her eyes and sat his "happy ass down."

"You think your pretty tough, don't you?" he said. This time he wasn't smiling.

"I learned from my dad. In fact if he knew that you made a play, he'd probably shoot your nuts off," Katie said.

"What do you want to know, bitch?" he said.

"That's better, asshole," she said. "Now, our investigation has made contact with the spirits in this building."

"Bullshit," Jasper said.

"I hope you're going to like Vienna," Katie said. "Now shut up and answer my questions."

"You want me to believe that you weirdos are on the level and speak to spirits?" he said.

"I don't care what you believe," Katie said.

"I don't have to say anything," Jasper said.

"Fine, you can just listen," Katie said. She closed her eyes and said, "Is that you, Holly? Holly Massey is that you? I want you to tell me what you remember when you were in the Studio program." There was silence in the room for a few minutes. Then Katie opened her eyes and looked directly into Jasper 's eyes. "You bastard, you seduced that girl. You told her that you could help her career, you used her."

Jasper laughed. "I've seen better performances at a carnival."

"What's that, Holly, they took you up to the fifth floor and they took turns raping you? You said they, who was the other person?" There was silence, then Katie said surprised, "His son." She looked at Jasper and asked do you have a son?"

"No," he said.

"Wait a minute," Katie said, "not his son, but, oh my God, Fontane's son. Who's that? Ashley Hodges, you too?" Hold on, who is contacting me--Abby. Abby, what's your last name? LaSalle? Do you remember either of these women?"

Jasper shook his head no.

Katie looked above Jasper and remained silent, she looked as if she were listening to someone whisper in her ear, then she spoke, "Jasper, they say you're a liar, they say you destroyed their lives, they say there will be revenge." Katie closed her eyes and was listening to the "spirits." She opened her eyes and smiled. "They have asked me to tell you, sweet dreams, Jasper."

Jasper was shaken. "What does that mean?"

"I don't know," Katie said, "but I'm guessing you're not going to get much sleep from here on out."

Katie stood up and smiled and left the room.

As she walked down the hall her phone rang. She answered, it was Greg.

"For the best creepy performance of 2022 the prize goes to Katie 'I'll kick your nuts up into your throat' Reed!" Greg laughed, "Do you think he bought it?"

Katie laughed. "I don't know, but I think I gave him something to think about."

"Pop will be so proud." Greg laughed.

"Did you guys see it?" Katie asked.

"Hell yes, we have cameras everywhere. I think Cal put a little scare into Ava. We're recording all the interviews, but this was the best. Casey suggested that tonight when you all get back, we get popcorn and watch all of them."

"I've finished all my interviews, is Cal done yet?" Katie asked.

"Cal finished a while go," Greg said.

"So, all the interviews are done," Katie said.

"Not quite, there is one left," Greg said.

"Who?" Katie asked.

"René Moreau," Greg said.

"I thought Cal was going to do that one. He got along with him pretty well," Katie said.

"He did, but Bart thought it would be a good idea to have someone else do it," Greg said.

"Who? Oh no, don't tell me Pop's going to do it." Katie laughed.

"Who else?" Greg said.

"Well, the weirder they are, the better Pops likes it," Katie said. "When is the interview?"

"In about a half hour," Greg said.

"Great, I'm going to find Cal and try to get back to watch it with you guys," Katie said.

"You better hurry because it's going to be standing room only," Greg said. "Sinclair, T.R. and the Chief are already up here and have front row seats. Baron and Ruby are sitting in front of the screen too. This is going to be weird versus weird."

Katie said, "My money is on the wolverine, Go Blue!"

Chapter 47

René Moreau was in his office; the door was closed. Nick knocked and heard Moreau call to him to enter.

Nick entered the room. It was lit by candles that were placed in front of the statues of the saints. He also had a stand of votive candles.

"Am I disturbing you?" Nick asked.

"Oh no," he said, "it's close to six and I was praying the Angelus. I pray it three times a day."

"We rarely see that kind of commitment these days," Nick said.

"For me it is the least I can do. Our Lady was without sin and an example to all of us. I pray it so that Our Lady will protect all our young women," Moreau said. "Are you a religious man, Professor?"

"Not as much as I should be, "Nick said, "but I do pray often."

"That's an honest answer," Moreau answered. "How may I help you?"

"My associate that spoke with you…"

"Al," Moreau said.

"That's correct," Nick said. "He was quite moved by your dedication to your dancers and your concern about their welfare."

"They come to us to learn the dance. They should be allowed to concentrate on the dance, the joy of the dance and the spiritual purity of the dance without the concern or fear for the temptations that can sully or tarnish their effort," Moreau said. "Throughout the scriptures dance and music have been a gift that is given to celebrate God."

Nick looked around the office. "You have some beautiful things here."

180

"Thank you," Moreau said. "I have been collecting them for years. That kneeler at one time was in the sacristy at the Cathedral."

"Really?" Nick said.

"Oh yes, it was given to me by Bishop Aymond twenty years ago," Moreau said with pride. "He is a fine man and a dedicated servant of Our Lord."

"How did you collect so much beautiful statuary?" Nick asked.

"I have been very fortunate to have had the opportunity to travel, Professor," he answered.

"Is this St. Martin de Pores?" Nick asked.

"Yes, I was able to purchase that in Spain. You will probably know who this saint is," Moreau said.

"Of course, you've done some research, I wouldn't be much of a professor at the school I teach at if I didn't recognize him, the soldier, St. Ignatius de Loyola," Nick said.

"I procured that in Spain as well," Moreau said. "I found St. Rose in Peru. Would you like to guess where in Peru?"

"I will take a wild guess; could it be Lima?" Nick laughed.

"Yes, it was," Moreau said, smiling.

"This one I don't recognize?" Nick said.

Moreau smiled and said, "What kind of choreographer would I be if I didn't include him?"

"Not St. Vitas?" Nick asked.

"Very good," Moreau said.

Nick looked at the statue of Mary Magdalen. It was three and half feet high and the centerpiece of Moreau's collection. It stood on a six-inch wooden stand on a table. "I am curious why Mary Magdalen is the most prominent work of art in your collection?"

"She is, after the Lord's mother, the most important woman in the Bible, despite the distortion of her memory,"

Moreau said. "She was not a prostitute. That was a myth perpetrated by the Church to diminish her importance."

Nick said, "She was a victim of a conspiracy?"

"I believe she was. There were many Marys in the Bible. I believe she was purposely misidentified because the Church could not have a woman seen as an important part of Christ's ministry," Moreau said. "Magdala was a Jewish village in Galilee. She was pure, and some believe that her family was wealthy and contributed to the ministry."

"Interesting," Nick said.

"She is also the patron saint of women," Moreau said, "so she is an inspiration."

"René, may I call you René?" Nick asked.

"Of course, Professor," Moreau said.

Nick said, "Well, René why don't you call me Nicholas."

"Certainly, Pro.., Nicholas," Moreau said.

"I have to ask for your help," Nick said.

"Anything," Moreau replied.

"Have you been threatened by anyone here at the Studio?"

"I am not sure that I have been threatened, but I guess you could say that I have been bullied," he said.

Nick asked, "By whom?"

"I would rather not say," Moreau said.

"Let me go about this in a different way," Nick said. "René, there are spirits in this building and Professor Bartholomew has been communicating with them."

"I am not surprised," Moreau said.

"That's right, I understand you too have communicated with the spirits," Nick said.

"Spirit," Moreau said, "one spirit."

"Have you identified the spirit?" Nick asked.

"Yes," Moreau said.

"Is that spirit Deidra Stewart?" Nick asked.

Moreau looked surprised.

182

"Jonathan Bartholomew has also been communicating with her and others as well," Nick said. "They have related information that is troubling about sexual abuse, and other criminal behavior that led to their death."

Moreau looked down. "I'm not surprised."

"René, is that why you have tirelessly tried to protect the young women here?"

"I tried but failed. It was all our responsibility to protect them," Moreau said. "It's my fault."

"Your fault?" Nick said.

"Yes, I tried to protect them," Moreau said. "I tried to warn them, but many were so fixated on their careers they became easy targets, and many young women were compromised and led into temptation."

"René, do you know who did this?" Nick asked.

Moreau looked at him.

"René, was it Jasper and Ti?"

"Those girls were pure and just wanted to be dancers," Moreau said.

"I wasn't going to share this information with anyone yet, but I believe that I can trust you and you must not share anything that I tell you with anyone, and I mean this must stay between us only. I haven't even told Jonathan this. Can you keep what I am about to tell you confidential, as it is vitally important? Can you promise me you will?"

"I promise," Moreau said.

"The New Orleans Police have gotten wind of our paranormal investigation. They have several cold cases about missing or deceased women that they suspect had ties to the studio. They have been embarrassed that they have not been able to close these cases for years. They have no confirmation, but the time frame has led them to believe that they have two suspects within the studio. I don't think I need to tell you who they suspect.

"From going over their investigations and interviews with the families of the missing or deceased women, they

183

believe they have learned that many of the women not only had a connection with the studio, but those that are deceased had identifiable personal items missing.

"They have concluded that there may be a serial killer at work. From the remains recovered there was not sufficient or identifiable DNA to identify the perpetrator or perpetrators. It is only a matter of time before they get a warrant to search the studio and interrogate everyone who works here or has worked here during the period they're looking at, and that period is at least the last two decades. At some point they will want to talk to you, and they are going to ask you about Jasper and Ti. My guess is that they will be looking for those missing personal items.

"That's why it is important that you not say anything. They don't want to tip off anyone who might be involved like Ti and Jasper. You understand?"

A shaken Moreau said, "I do."

"When I heard what the police were planning and heard from Al how you challenged Jasper and demanded that interviews be chaperoned, I became concerned for you," Nick said.

"Concerned for me? Why?" Moreau asked.

"TI and Jasper are assholes; I've gotten into it with them about our paranormal investigation. I got this horrible feeling that If word got out about the police getting involved they might try to shift the blame by framing someone and I thought that because you cared so much about the women and you had the courage to stand up to them, you might be the logical person they might try to frame. I wanted to give you a heads up, so that you can be on guard."

"Thank you, Nicholas, I will be vigilant, and I won't say a word to anyone."

"Standing up and confronting them took courage and honor," Nick said. "I have to get back and work on the paranormal report with Jonathan. I will check in with you tomorrow."

+

In the car on his way back to Sinclair's, Nick called Greg. "Make sure the surveillance on the offices are monitored all the time. I'm on my way back."

Chapter 48

Jasper burst into Ava's office. "What the flying..."

"What?" Ava responded.

"Get Ti down here, now," he said.

"What, now?" she said.

"We're screwed, those ghostbuster bastards are on the level. They know something," he said.

"Ti, you better get down here, your buddy is cracking up," Ava said.

"They know," Jasper said.

"They know what?" Ava said.

Ti said, "They know nothing," as he came through the door. "Now calm down."

"I am telling you, the paranormal people know about the girls," Jasper said.

"Get a hold of yourself. They can't and don't know anything. How would they know?" Ti said.

"They were told," Jasper said.

"They were told, who would or could tell anyone? No one knows but the tree of us," Ti said, "and what would they tell them?"

Jasper looked down and said, "A ghost told them."

"Excuse me, did you just say a ghost told them? You're losing it."

Jasper replied, "No, I'm not, they know something. I think they know what we did, and I think they believe we had something to do with what happened to those girls."

"What we did? We didn't do anything," Ti said.

"I guess you're not counting getting them drunk, or slipping them a little Ecstasy, LSD, or Ketamine," Ava said.

"No one can prove that we did that," Ti said, "and we didn't kill anyone."

"You sure about that?" Ava said.

"When we were done with them, they were alive and sleeping it off on the fifth floor or in the basement," Ti said.

"But as I recall, dear, you're the one that came to us all stressed that one was dead and demanded that we had to help you get rid of the body. You always found them and told us how to dispose of the problem. Jasper and I didn't initiate it. Oh, get over them, do you have a count?"

"I was protecting you and the studio," Ava said. "I was protecting what your father built and what you and your dumb ass sidekick tried to destroy every chance you could. I did what was necessary."

"You didn't answer my question," Ti said, "how many."

Ava glared at him and said, "Around nineteen."

Jasper said, "What? Nineteen?

"Time flies when you're having fun," Ti said.

"You know, Ava," Ti began, "it's funny that when Jasper and I left them they were alive."

"That's right," Jasper said, jumping in. "We didn't kill them or decide they needed to disappear."

"You didn't help them along a little, did you, Ava?" Ti asked.

"You son of a bitch," Ava said.

"No reason to get upset. I'm just asking a question," Ti said.

"I would never do anything like that," she protested.

"I'm sorry, I forgot what an altruistic saint you are," Ti said. "It won't be long until that little creep René has a statue of you in his office: St. Ava, patron saint of the cleanup in isle four."

"Rot in hell," Ava said.

"I probably will, but let's get one thing clear. If one of us goes down, we will all go down," Ti said. "You two got that?"

+

"Nick, get up here, you have to see this," Felix said, "part one worked."

"What about part two?" Nick asked.

"We got that too," Felix said. "While they were at each other's throats, the part two setup went down."

"Good, you have that recorded too?"

"We do," Felix said.

"Let Bart know," Nick said. "You and Greg did a great job on this."

Chapter 49

They all sat around the large table in the ballroom: Nick and Bart at one end of the table; the Chief and Lucas Bryant at the other end; Sinclair, T. R., Felix, Greg and Casey filling the rest of the chairs.

"Greg, play it," Nick said.

They watched the first video in silence. When it was finished, Chief Bryant spoke. "Nick, it's a little thin, they don't admit to the assaults or rapes, and certainly the murders or even kidnapping would be tough to prove. We can probably get all three for unlawful disposal of the bodies."

Lucas spoke up. "They did admit to disposing of nineteen bodies, Chief, couldn't a case be made for murder. I mean nineteen, for God's sake."

"If they had a good lawyer and all we have is the video," T.R. said, "I don't think you could get a conviction, you need more."

"Felix, what about DNA or blood evidence from the fifth floor or basement area?" the Chief asked.

"There was some blood, but after all these years and the condition of both spaces it was degraded to the point where we would have difficulty getting a blood type, same with DNA," Felix said.

"The difficulty here is that we have no survivors," Chief Bryant said.

"What about the women on the list whose remains were recovered and underwent an autopsy?" Sinclair asked.

"There are six," Casey said. "We have reports on all of them and all six had traces of either Ecstasy, LSD, or Ketamine. Also, in four of the women there was a high content of alcohol."

"If we can connect the drugs to Ti, Jasper or Ava, we may have something," Lucas said.

"There are a lot of 'ifs' here. Most everything is circumstantial and since all this happened over a long period, that makes it very difficult. We could get them on desecration of a corpse, possibly a felony but murder.... If we can connect them with the drugs, maybe date rape or assault, but it would be weak, "Chief Bryant said.

"Casey, tell everyone what the cause of death was for the six women we have reports on," Nick said.

"Suffocation or strangulation," she replied.

"So, what we're saying is that Ti and Jasper drugged them, assaulted or raped them, then murdered them by strangling them, then with Ava got rid of the bodies," T.R. said, "and they did this nineteen times."

"This is going to be a bitch to sell to a prosecutor," Chief Bryant said. "Nick, what the hell?"

"I never promised you an airtight case," Nick said. "Why don't we watch the second video. Greg run it."

"What are we watching here?" Chief Bryant asked.

"What the hell is he doing?" Lucas asked.

"Never mind," Nick said, "wait for it."

"Is that a cabinet?" Sinclair asked.

"Sort of," Nick said.

"Is that what I think it is?" Bart asked, as the person on the screen pulled out a small wooden box.

"I don't know yet but keep on watching," Nick said.

The surveillance video followed the person with the box down the hallway to another office where the person opened the door and entered. The person went to a four-drawer file cabinet and opened the bottom drawer and placed the box in the drawer at the back. They closed the drawer and left the office, then walked back to the elevator, exited the elevator on the main floor, and left the building.

"What did we just see and what's in the box?" the Chief asked.

"We saw someone who was getting even," Nick said. "They were framing someone to misdirect our attention from them."

"Whose office did they put the box in?" Lucas asked.

"That would be Ti Barbeau's office," Nick said.

Nick's cell buzzed. "Well," he said.

"Constance and Bob are on it. Looks like your friend is heading home. I'm entering the office now," Cal said.

Nick put the phone on speaker. The sound of a file drawer opening could be heard. Then Cal came back on the line, "Bingo and it's in there."

"Put it back," Nick said, "and come on back."

"See you soon," Cal said, "as soon as the calvary gets here."

"Okay, Nick, what was in the box?" Chief Bryant asked.

"First, could Sergeant Bryant make a call and get a couple of officers over there to ensure the chain of custody?" Nick asked. We have the surveillance video, but back up would be nice."

Lucas rose and left the room to make the call.

Nick continued, "Several of the victim's families of the missing and deceased young women told us that there were items missing when their loved one's body was found. Cal just confirmed that those items are in the box."

Nick turned to Sinclair, "Deidra's locket was there," Nick said.

Sinclair looked down. T.R. put his hand on his friend's shoulder, and both men had tears in their eyes. Nick looked at the chief who wiped a tear from his eye.

Nick continued, "We looked all over the place for that box and couldn't find it. We thought it might be in the basement or on the fifth floor which is where most of the assaults were committed, and we think the murders."

"How did you know the box was still in the building?" T.R. asked.

"We got a couple of anonymous tips; it will be in the unofficial report we submit to you," Nick said.

The chief nodded. This was New Orleans, after all. "Well, I guess we should go pick up a few folks this evening."

"Chief, I need a favor," Nick said.

"Name it," he replied.

"Could we wait until tomorrow?" Nick asked.

He continued, "Well, I think I owe it to Fontaine to talk to him in the morning and let him know what we have really been doing, and we're going to give the paranormal report in the afternoon to him and the rest of his staff."

T.R. said, "Nick, don't tell me you're going to do a 'Thin Man' on them."

"Okay, I'm not going to tell you that," Nick said." Bart..."

"He's going to do a 'Thin Man' on them," Bart said.

"Nick, really?" the chief said.

"Bart..." Nick said.

"Really," Bart said.

"Do you two rehearse this stuff," T.R. asked.

"If you let me do this by tomorrow afternoon, I think I can get a confession from the murderer, and from Ti, Jasper and Ava," Nick said.

"We still have a weak case on the assaults," Chief Bryant said.

"Maybe not," Nick said. "Casey, could you please bring our friend in?"

"She's down the hall with Katie and Alana, playing with Baron and Ruby," she said and left the room.

"Chief, could you take off your jacket?" Nick asked.

"My Jacket?" he replied.

"Yes, please, if Baron comes in and sees the uniform, he might think you're a postman," Nick said.

The chief slipped off his jacket with a laugh.

Baron and Ruby burst into the ballroom. Baron looked at the chief and hopped up into the chair next to him, sniffed his hand and licked it. He then sat straight up looking like he could be part of the chief's staff. The chief laughed. Ruby jumped up into Sinclair's lap.

Casey walked in followed by Alex Hicks.

"May I present Ms. Alex Hicks, Fontaine Barbeau's gatekeeper and the inside operative for Caldwell & Cheswick Investigations. Ms. Hicks wants a career in law enforcement and investigations. She has something for us that we could not have gotten without her help," Nick said. "Alex, this is Chief Bryant, T.R. Bryant, Sinclair Stewart, and Sergeant Lucas Bryant, all detectives, Felix Coughlin, forensics, and I think you have met Greg Wells."

Alex blushed.

"Give us your report, Ms. Hicks," Nick said.

"I did a background check on Professor Neff and Dr. Bartholomew and found that they were really Mr. Caldwell and Mr. Cheswick. I did not disclose this to anyone. I made Mr. Caldwell aware of this and asked if I could help. He didn't know how I could but said it would be good if I heard anything that could help the investigation. I didn't but I knew most of the disappearances and deaths were cold cases and would be difficult to solve. I also knew about the behavior patterns of Ti Barbeau and Jasper Marchal firsthand.

"I came to the studio to study dance and was harassed by Ti and Jasper and quit my dance program. Mr. Fontaine offered me a position with the studio. I also knew there were other dancers who were being harassed and threatened that they would lose their places in the dance company if they did not comply with the requests of Ti and Jasper.

"I decided to talk with the girls who had been pressured that I knew about. I found seven, three of which that had been assaulted and four that they tried to pressure. Those four withdrew from the Studio.

"I secured notarized statements from each girl." Alex handed folders to the chief and Nick. "These young women, particularly the three that were assaulted were afraid. We all knew the rumors about the women who disappeared or died. I told them that the pressure would never stop unless we came forward. All of us were afraid. Mr. Caldwell directed me to work with Casey and Phil Caldwell. I hope that this will be helpful in the investigation. The studio is a wonderful place and Mr. Fontaine Barbeau is a good man. He deserves better and so do the dancers in the company."

"Thank you, Alex," Nick said.

The chief was looking at the affidavits. "Ms. Hicks, this is good work."

"Thank you, sir," Alex said.

"Ms. Hicks, we will interview the women. At first look, I believe this will be helpful to our investigation," the chief said. "Oh, Ms. Hicks, when you complete your schooling, if you still want to pursue a career in law enforcement, contact me." The chief gave her his card.

"I will, sir, thank you again," she said.

"Casey, take Alex and introduce her to the rest of our people," Nick said.

As they left, Baron licked the chief's hand and ran out of the room with Ruby following Casey and Alex.

"This information establishes a pattern of behavior, and I would not be surprised if others come forward after these young women are interviewed," Nick said.

"It gives us some leverage we didn't have before, that's for sure," the chief said.

"Two things, Nick, first do the show tomorrow," Chief Bryant said.

"Thank you," Nick said.

"I will have warrants for the search, and I will have officers at the studio in place," Chief Bryant said. "What time is your meeting with Fontaine?"

"Eleven," Nick said.

"Good, we can meet at my office at nine to go over the details," he said.

"That works for us," Nick said, "What was the second thing, Chief?"

"If Alex goes to the academy and we train her, you have to promise me you won't hire her away from us too soon," Chief Bryant said.

Nick smiled. "Chief, I can't make promises I'm not sure I can keep."

Chapter 50

It was after midnight when Nick walked through the front door of the studio. He nodded to the maintenance crew, who were New Orleans police this evening.

"Mr. Caldwell, everything okay?" the officer asked.

"As well as can be expected," Nick responded. "Could you open the door to the theatre; I have to do a presentation tomorrow and I want to get a feel for the room."

"Not a problem, is there anything I can help you with?" the officer asked.

"No, I just want to go in and think a little bit," Nick said, "but thank you."

The theatre was dark with the usual exception of the "Ghost Light" that was set in the middle of the stage. In fact, every theatre leaves a "Ghost Light" on when the theatre isn't occupied. Nick smiled thinking about how appropriate that is.

He walked down the steps of the teacup theatre and sat in the center section on the aisle. He focused on the "Ghost Light."

"I know you're here, Deidra," he said.

He saw a young woman on the stage rehearsing a dance.

"Aren't you a clever detective," she said.

"Yes, I am," Nick said.

"Tomorrow is the big day," she said. "I'm proud of you, figuring it out and all."

"Thank you," Nick said,

"Nick, Nick, Nick, I heard you're doing a 'Thin Man' on them. Nicky, Nicky, Nicky," she said.

"What's with the Nick, Nick, Nick thing?" He asked.

"I'm trying to be Myrna Loy to your William Powell, your Nora Charles to Nick Charles," she said as she continued dancing.

"Myrna Loy never said that to Powell. It was used on the National Lampoon Radio Hour in the seventies in a sketch called 'Nick Danger, Third Eye and he had a Duck that went quack, quack..." Nick said.

"The seventies? Well, you would know, old timer." Then she laughed.

"So, to what do I owe this visit?" she asked.

"We're almost to the end of the case and to the end of this little dance you and I have going," he said.

"I'm disappointed, I thought you came by to catch a look at me in tights," she said, with a giggle.

"See, that's what I mean. I came here to let you know about the case," Nick said.

"Nick, do think Dad would shoot you if he knew you were scoping out my legs?" She laughed again.

"Will you give it a rest, and yes he probably would," Nick said.

"Aren't you afraid that your girlfriend would be jealous if she knew you were here giving me the once over?" she said.

"There you go again," he said. "This is the dance I'm talking about, and Casey is not my girlfriend."

"I didn't mean Casey; I meant the other one. The one that I remind you of, the bad girl," Deidra said.

"I don't have a girlfriend," Nick said.

"I could be a bad girl," she said and laughed.

"You could also be alive, but you're not," Nick said.

"You know, Nick, you really know how to hurt a ghost," she said.

I just came by to see if there was anything else that you think I should know before the take down tomorrow?" Nick said.

"You came by to see if there is anything else you should know before a drawing room reveal tomorrow?" she said.

"Yes," Nick said.

"You mean besides how good I look in tights?" she said.

"Really?" Nick said. "Okay, it's late and I need to get some rest, I'm heading back."

"Wait," she said.

"What?" Nick said.

"When you have your meeting with Fontane..." she said.

"Yeah?" Nick asked.

"Be gentle with him, he may have suspected something was going on, but he wasn't involved at all," she said. "This is his son who is being taken down and the murder suspect has also been very loyal to him. Fontane is going to be shell shocked."

"Anything else?" Nick asked.

"You can get the confession. Your suspect is proud of what he does; it's his mission. He looks at this as necessary to purify us." she said.

"I'll do my best," Nick said.

"I know that. I have one more thing," she said. "Don't you think that Alex Hicks deserves her dream date with Greg?" she asked.

"Okay, I'll try," he said.

"And Nick, just a heads up," she said, "all of us will be here tomorrow."

"During the 'Thin Man'?" he asked, "where?"

"Center section, row G, seats 1-19. Could you get the row reserved?" she asked.

Nick said "Yes, I assume row G is for..."

"Ghosts, of course," she giggled.

"Of course," he said.

"it's been fun, Nick" she said, "except for all the murder stuff. I've enjoyed our, as you call it, our little dance."

"I'm glad I have had the chance to meet you, Deidra," Nick said.

"Hey, watch out for my dad. He thinks of you as the son he never had," she said.

"Goodnight," Nick said and began to walk toward the exit.

"Good night, Nick, and I know you were scoping me out," she said, with a laugh.

Nick sighed and headed for the door. As he got to it, Deidra began humming *I'll be Watching You* from the old song by the Police.

As Nick reached for the door, he called back to her, "Not funny, Deidra."

Chapter 51

The meeting started early.

Chief Bryant asked, "Nick, how do you see this going down?"

"Bart will give the paranormal report, then turn it over to me and I'll do what I do best," Nick said.

"You mean irritate and piss off people," Sinclair said. "That boy could have provoked Sister Teresa into taking a swing at him."

"Nick, could you be a little more specific?" Chief Bryant said.

"Sure, I let them know we know what they did, and we know they killed those girls. After what we saw on the video, they are ready to turn on each other, and they will. Lucas, you offer them the deal, first one to turn gets the deal, everybody else burns. I tell them I would like to see all of them charged with murder. Then I say they can't be charged with murder, and we explain why," Nick said. While all this is happening, NOLA PD is executing the search and you have officers at the exits.

"We get the confession, your folks come in and then you say, 'Cuff'em, Danno.' You get the credit for the bust.

"You meet with the prosecutor; we stick around for the arraignment. Then we have a party and take a few days for sightseeing. Then we leave town, but we will come back for the trial, if needed. Sound like a plan?"

"Anything else?" the Chief asked.

"Yeah," Nick said, "you get the trial during football season, and you get me tickets to see LSU and tickets for whatever weekend the Saints play Tampa Bay. And after the trial, I'll get tickets for you to see the Birmingham Barons and tickets for a Bears' game of your choice."

"The Birmingham Barons were Michael Jordan's old team," the chief said.

"It was also Reggie Jackson's, Rollie Fingers', Frank Thomas', Tony La Russa's and, wait for it, Willie Mays' old team," Nick said.

The chief started laughing. "Okay, Nick, it's a deal."

"So, what Bears' game do you want to see?" Nick asked.

The Chief smiled and said, "I think I will pass on the Bears' game."

"That's my team," Nick said.

"I know, and I can only say, I'm sorry for you," Chief Bryant replied and laughed.

"You really know how to hurt a guy," Nick said. Nick acted hurt and said, "I'm out of here; I have to go see a man and confess my dishonesty."

"Probably not the first time," Lucas said.

"Have a little respect for your elders youngin'." Nick gave Lucas a parking ticket and asked, "Can you take care of this?" Then he laughed, walked out, and headed for the studio.

Chapter 52

Nick and Bart got to Fontaine's office a little early. Alex Hicks was sitting in the outer office.

"Good morning, Professor Neth, Professor Bartholomew," she said.

"Not necessary today," Nick said, "we're here to come clean."

"Oh," she said. "He is waiting for you." Alex knocked on the door.

Fontaine called to her, "Alex, have them come in."

"Ah, gentlemen, the big day. Dr. Bartholomew, your report is completed?"

"It is," Bart said, "I hope you will be pleased."

"Dr. Neth, is your report complete?" he asked.

"My report?" Nick said, then he smiled.

Bart began, "His report..."

Nick interrupted. "Bart, save it, the Maestro knows. May I ask you a question before we apologize? How long have you known?"

"Only a few days, Nick. May I call you Nick?" Fontaine asked.

"You can call me anything you want to call me," Nick said. "I deceived you. What tipped you off?"

"Did I tell you that my darling little Alex and I share a common interest?" he said.

"No, you didn't," Nick said.

"We both revel and celebrate film noir, crime fiction and true crime novels. Every week for the past year she has urged me to read these books about this detective from Chicago, except the last few weeks. Since you've arrived, she hasn't mentioned those books at all," he said. "I read about two of these books every five days."

He opened his desk drawer. Nick hoped he wasn't going to bring out a gun, but he would not have blamed him.

Fontaine took out three books, *Justice Delayed, Not Forgotten,* and *Dead Crowe*."

"Can you get your money back?" Nick asked.

"I don't want my money back, I liked them," he said. "Have you read them?"

"Actually, I'm more of a Connelly, Hammett, and Chandler fan," Nick said.

Fontaine said, "I like them too, but you should really read these books. The main characters are very interesting. I particularly liked the older detective."

"The one from New Orleans," Fontaine continued, "he reminds me of an old friend."

"I know who you mean, but I thought he was a pain in the ass," Nick said.

Fontaine smiled and said, "So is my friend, but he is a good man who suffered a terrible tragedy, and he deserves justice. If I were him and had the connections with excellent detectives like yourself and Mr. Cheswick that specialize in cold cases, I would not hesitate to hire them to solve the case that destroyed my life."

"Who else in this building knows why we are here?" Nick asked.

"As far as I know just Alex and me," Fontaine said. "Nick, this studio is my life, it is my legacy, and now it has become my Denmark."

"Denmark?" Nick said.

"Are you familiar with *Hamlet*?" Fontaine asked.

"I've read the play and have seen the play and the film with Olivier," Nick said.

"Then you are probably familiar with the line, '*Something is rotten in the state of Denmark,*'" Fontaine said.

"I am," Nick said.

"Something is rotten in my studio," Fontaine said. "No matter where your investigation leads, I want those responsible for the tragedy that has befallen my life's work rooted out, destroyed, and punished. I want our reputation restored, no matter the cost. Do you understand?"

"I believe I do," Nick said.

"I believe you do, too, Fontaine said. "I look forward to your presentation this afternoon."

"Maestro, you are an honorable and good man," Nick said.

"Thank you, but not knowing and allowing the terrible things that were happening here to go on without being aware because I was preoccupied with the art, I will always feel like a narcissistic, ego centric old fool. I have not been a good steward or keeper of what I built and loved. I will carry this shame and guilt forever," he said and turned and looked out his window.

Nick and Bart rose and left the Maestro's office and headed to the theatre. Their silence was broken when Bart said "Wow."

"Yeah," Nick said, quietly.

Chapter 53

At eleven o'clock the entire senior staff of the studio was gathered in the theatre with the entire Caldwell/Cheswick staff and a few NOLA police officers to round it out. Chief Bryant was on hand as well. At the stroke of eleven, Chief Bryant Gave the order for all the exits to be closed and guarded and that the search warrants should be executed. Fontaine sat next to the Chief. A few minutes before eleven the Chief handed Fontaine the warrants as arranged, and Fontaine put them in his jacket pocket.

Nick stood in the middle of the stage with Bart next to him and began.

"Good morning, Nick said, "our job here is almost at an end, and for some of you I'm sure that is a relief. One of our tasks here was to investigate and verify whether there is paranormal activity in the studio and who these spirits might be. I will now turn it over to Bartholomew."

"Thank you, Nicholas. We conducted a thorough investigation using the most modern equipment available," Bart said.

From the back of the theatre, a voice yelled, "What, a Ouija Board?" It was Jasper.

"Not this time and I want to commend you for the originality of your comment. I've never heard that one before; it is truly clever and the product of a keen mind," Bart replied.

Many in the audience laughed, resulting in a scowl from Jasper.

Bart looked at Jasper and said, "May I continue?"

Jasper, looking and feeling like the horse's ass he was, remained silent.

"Good, I will continue," Bart said. "In a building as old as this and considering that this building over the years has been used in a variety of ways, we found that there was spiritual activity that spanned several centuries, and we were fortunate that they did communicate with our team. There were laborers who worked on the building. We also communicated with spirits who had associations with this building since it had become the dance studio. Their stories were different; they did not die accidently, as many of the workman did, but they were murdered."

A gasp came from the audience.

"All of these spirits were the young women who had been in the dance program. There were nineteen," Bart said. "Before they met their end, they were all assaulted, bullied, forced to do unmentionable things. Then they were murdered."

There was an uneasiness that swept the theatre and there was dead silence.

"At this time, I will turn the presentation over to Nicholas," Bart said.

Nick looked up at the center section, row G and seats one through nineteen and realized that all twenty seats were occupied. In seat twenty he saw Sinclair and in seat nineteen was Deidra. She had her arm around her dad, and she was smiling, as were the other eighteen women. Nick wondered if anyone else saw them.

"Thank you, Bart, and I would like to thank all of you that cooperated with the investigation, especially Maestro Fontaine Barbeau."

"I have a confession to make," Nick said. "We came to New Orleans because we were engaged by a client who wanted us to investigate the murder of his daughter. I am not a professor of historical architecture. My name is Nick Caldwell, and I am a private detective, as is Bart Cheswick. Bart is also a psychologist and a paranormal investigator. Our main office is in Chicago, and we have other offices in Saint Louis and here in New Orleans.

"Everything Bart told you is true. We gained useful information from his investigation."

Nick noticed that Ti, Jasper, and Ava were squirming a little in their seats; he thought they should be, but they hadn't heard anything yet.

"Once we realized the extent and magnitude of the situation, we immediately contacted the New Orleans Police Department and Chief Bryant. The chief is sitting with Maestro Fontaine. We have been cooperating and working with him through most of this investigation.

"The NOLA PD has supported our investigation and launched an investigation of their own. That has brought us here today. They secured warrants for surveillance so that any information or evidence that we uncovered would be admissible in a court of law. At this moment a search warrant has been executed to search this building and their officers are posted at every exit in this building and at every exit of this theatre. The chief has graciously allowed me to present our findings."

Ti noticed that there were officers at both ends of the row where he, Jasper and Ava were sitting.

"We have found that nineteen young women who were murdered, as mentioned, were students and part of the dance company at one time," Nick said. "They were seduced, assaulted and raped. They were lured to their deaths with the promise to be helped in their pursuit of a dance career or by the threat that their careers would be destroyed. They were bullied, assaulted and broken. After these assaults we believe they were threatened that more harm might come to them if they spoke about it to anyone. Then they were killed. Their remains were then removed to cover up what had been done to them. Some of them have been found, some are still missing.

"You may ask how could this happen, how is this possible? I asked these questions myself. These young women were just that, young, ambitious, inexperienced, and they trusted the people whom they believed would help them achieve their dreams of becoming professional dancers.

But they put their trust in vile predators, who lied to them, manipulated them and used them and they paid a price they did not deserve. They were not the only ones. There are seven young women who have come forward who escaped their fate and are being interviewed by the NOLA PD."

The theatre was silent.

"We interviewed the families of the deceased and missing women and found that in most of these cases there were personal items that were important to these women that were not recovered. These items were dear to them, such as jewelry. We believe that these were souvenirs taken by the killer or killers."

Nick looked up at the chief. The chief nodded.

"The NOLA PD has recovered these items," Nick said.

There was a nervous energy that rolled through like a giant wave.

Nick looked at three people and said, "So, Ti, Jasper and Ava, what do you think, did I get it right?"

The air seemed to rush from the room, followed by a chatter and cries.

Ti stood up and said, "You son of a bitch, we didn't do anything."

"How can you spread such a lie," Ava said. "This is outrageous, I will sue you for defamation."

Jasper shouted, "I didn't kill anyone, besides they wanted it."

The room fell silent, and Ava and Ti looked at Jasper like he might be the next murder victim at the studio.

"Did I accuse you of anything?" Nick asked. "I certainly did not accuse you of murder, even though the police did find the missing personal items in one of your offices."

"That's impossible," Ti said, "you are trying to fame us."

"What am I trying to frame you for?" Nick said.

"The murders," Ava exploded.

"I'm not trying to frame you for the murders," Nick said. "The items were found in Jasper's office."

Ti looked at Jasper, went to grab him, yelling, "You stupid asshole, I'll kill you."

An officer pulled Ti off Jasper but not in time to stop Ava from landing a solid right cross square on Jasper's jaw. Another officer pulled her off Jasper when she tried to punch him again. The officers subdued them and sat them back in their seats.

"Jasper," Nick said, "How did those items get into your office?"

"I don't know, I swear I didn't kill anyone. I don't know how they got there." Jasper said. "One of them must have put them there."

"Okay," Nick said, "which one?"

"I don't know," Jasper said."

"Which one do think was trying to frame you, Ti or Ava?" Nick asked.

"She was the one that found them," he said.

"You are a disgusting, gutless worm. I'm not the one that screwed them," Ava said, "you did."

Jasper said, "We didn't kill them, we may have…"

Ti screamed, "Will you just shut the fuck up."

"It was your idea. You're the one who likes the young ones," Jasper said.

"Everyone calm down," Nick said. "Whether or not you killed them, if I had my way, you all deserve the needle. You are barely human debris. Regardless of whether you killed them, they are dead because of the position you put them in. I'm not an advocate of capital punishment, but for the three of you, I'd make an exception.

"What you did was bad enough, but you're technically not guilty of murder. You didn't kill them," Nick continued, "Did they René?."

"What," René said, nervously.

"Ti, Jasper and Ava defiled these young women, destroyed their purity and once they lost their virtue and succumbed to temptation they were lost. Their souls were lost. They had sinned and turned away from the righteous path of the Savior. They would have been condemned to everlasting suffering in hell with no hope of salvation," Nick said. "Isn't that true?"

"It is, Nick," René said.

"You cared for and loved these girls. You wanted them to have the attributes of St. Rose and St. Olga. You wanted them to respect their talent like St. Vitas. You wanted them to have the strength and integrity of Loyola and St. Martin, but most of all you didn't want them to carry the stigma that the Magdalene had to carry through history, did you," Nick said.

"Yes, Nick, I knew you would understand," René said.

"You wanted to save them to lead them to salvation. They had sinned and their penance was to repent and be sacrificed and become martyrs so that they could enter the kingdom," Nick said.

"They have entered the kingdom because of their sacrifice, Nick," René said.

"After you helped them make their sacrifice, you would take something dear to them and place it in a box and put it in the base of the Magdalene's statue so that they would be close to her, but it couldn't end there, could it, René. The evil doers needed to be exposed and punished for their sins. You had tried to stop them by insisting that there would be chaperones whenever they were in contact with the evil doers."

"I tied, Nick," René said.

"I know you did, René," Nick said. "That is why you took the box from the base of the statue and put it in Jasper's office, because you knew he was weak, and he would break, and he would turn on the others and they would turn on him, and their sins would be discovered, and they would be punished."

"They turned on each other like vipers. They will be punished, won't they, Nick?" René asked.

"They will, René," Nick said, "in this world and probably the next."

René smiled and said, "Thy will be done on earth as it is in heaven."

A man stood next to Nick. Nick turned and introduced him. "René, this is Father Gibbons. He is the chaplain for the New Orleans Police Department, and he would like to pray with you."

"Would that be all right with you?" Nick asked.

"I'd like that, Nick, thank you," René said. "I knew when I met you that you were a good man."

"Thank you," Nick said, "I try."

"You are very kind, I knew you would understand," René said.

"René, I don't," Nick said. "Go with Father Gibbons; he's a good man."

René looked confused but smiled and said, "May God bless you." Father Gibbons took René's arm and led him out of the theatre.

Chapter 54

The theatre was empty. The Ghost Light was center stage.

Nick sat alone, center section, row G seat 20, on the aisle.

All the perps were in custody. All the police were gone. All the Studio staff were given the rest of the day off. All the Caldwell-Cheswick investigators were probably at Pat O'Brian's or some other place in the Quarter. Sinclair went home. He said he wanted some quality time with Baron and Ruby. Fontaine and Trip went home trying to understand why and how Ti could do the things he did. Tomorrow Felix, Cal and Greg would come to the studio and pack up all the surveillance equipment, and the rest of the staff would pack up everything at Sinclair's.

He felt relieved that this case was over. They would stay in New Orleans a few more days if they wanted to, but he was pretty sure that Bart, Constance, Felix and Bob would leave for Chicago tomorrow. He had seen Greg talking to Alex Hicks and he thought that Greg would be sticking around New Orleans for a few more days to make sure that all the equipment and files were "packed properly." He was sure that Alex Hicks would volunteer to help him.

He knew that Katie, Phil, Alana, Casey and Cal were planning a surprise for Sinclair. Then they would head back to Chicago, except for Phil and Casey, who would go to Saint Louis to keep the office open and wait to hear what the future would be for the Saint Louis office.

He didn't know where he would be going--Chicago, Saint Louis, maybe Ann Arbor. He was always relaxed up there. He had always toyed with the idea of an office there.

He had dreaded this moment from the time Sinclair called and he and Phil rushed down here. What would he do next. He didn't have a plan; he wasn't sure he wanted to go back to Chicago full time or split the time and go to Saint Louis.

He was exhausted; he just wanted to sit in the dark theatre for a while with his eyes closed and try not to think about anything.

"Rough day, big boy?"

"Don't you have some ghost stuff to do?" he said.

"Don't you have some alive stuff to do?" Deidra said.

"No, I just wanted a little quiet," Nick said.

"Well, it's quiet here," she said.

"It was," he said.

"You did a good job, Nick," she said.

"It was a team effort," he said.

"What do you think will happen?" she asked.

"What do you mean?" Nick asked.

"To the bad guys, duh," she said.

"I think Ti and Jasper will do some serious time. Ava will go away for a while and if anyone can go for an insanity plea, René can," Nick said.

"What about Fontaine? she asked.

"He'll have a broken heart and feel guilty he raised a sociopath. He's lucky he still has Trip. I think they will put all this back together," Nick said.

"I hope so," she said. "Do you think Dad will be okay?"

"Your dad is one of--if not the--toughest men I know. He will never get over losing you and your mom, but as long as he lives, he'll keep fighting the good fight," Nick said. "What are your plans?"

"I thought I might just stick around and haunt you," she said.

"Please don't, having you around is exhausting," Nick said.

"I'm going to stay around here. Maybe I'll haunt Dad," she said.

"He'd like that," Nick said.

"He needs someone to watch over him," she said.

"Everyone does," Nick said.

"You do," she said.

"I do what, need someone to watch over me or have someone watching over me?" Nick said, with a laugh.

"You have someone. Mary and Wil are never that far away from you, and neither is that brown and black mutt," she said.

"Duke?" Nick asked.

"I'm sure Baron sees him. He thinks Duke is his dad," she laughed. "You owe that dog."

"Don't I know it," Nick said.

"Why are you hanging around here?" Nick asked. "I hope not for my sake."

"Don't get your hopes up, no peep show for you tonight." She laughed.

"Please don't start that stuff again," Nick said.

"I'm not here for you, I'm here for them, open your eyes, chump," she said.

Nick opened his eyes. On stage were eighteen young women, all were smiling.

"What's this about?" Nick said.

"They wanted to thank you," Deidra said, "so don't be a jerk and just accept it."

Each woman filed in front of Nick and smiled, and he could feel their gratitude. They didn't speak, but he felt a warmth as they passed by.

"Now say, you're welcome, Bozo," Deidra said.

"You're welcome," Nick said.

He blinked and Deidra and he were alone in the theatre.

"You did a great job, for a Sam Spade wanna be," she said, smiling.

"Thanks," he said, "I guess our dance is officially over now."

"For now, you never know. Who knows another time, another life…another dimension, you may fall for my charms," Deidra said.

"Really?" Nick said, with a hint of sarcasm.

"Really," she said with more than a hint of determination.

She smiled and faded away.

Nick laughed and said to himself, "I will be glad when I get out of New Orleans. This place is way too weird for me."

"You could get used to it," he heard her say.

"You always have to have the last word, don't you," he said.

"Yep."

Chapter 55

The next morning the New Orleans Police Department held its press conference.

Chief Bryant invited Nick to take part in the conference. Nick was not excited about this. He didn't like press conferences; he didn't like publicity and he didn't like the press at all.

It began promptly at nine. Everything Chief Bryant did began promptly, which is probably why he is the chief.

"Good morning. Yesterday afternoon the New Orleans police executed warrants to search the Barbeau Dance Studio. At the time of the search a presentation was conducted and during that presentation four persons of interest were taken into custody involving a cold case that has been open over the last two decades. The case dealt with the disappearance and murders of nineteen young women. You will receive at the end of this conference information on the alleged victims.

"This investigation was conducted in an unusual partnership with the Chicago-based investigative firm, Caldwell & Cheswick Investigations. I would like to introduce Nicholas Caldwell, partner and lead investigator for the firm. Nick…"

"Thank you, Chief Bryant," Nick said. "Approximately three weeks ago we were contacted by the family of one of the murdered women. They asked us, because of our experience with cold case investigations, to become involved.

"We made the decision to conduct the investigation as an undercover investigation. We quickly determined that we should contact Chief Bryant and brief him on what we knew and what we believed. We were planning to turn the investigation over to the New Orleans Police Department, but the chief proposed a partnership. We were eager to continue the case, and because of Chief Bryant's reputation as a no-nonsense police officer we were eager to assist him in any

216

way he thought appropriate. It was determined by the Chief and the New Orleans Police Department that we would serve in information gathering, initial interviewing staff and potential suspects and surveillance activities. The police secured the proper and needed warrants and we conducted surveillance activities and interviews and the initial forensic investigation.

"Once we entered the partnership, we turned over all evidence, video interviews and surveillance material to the New Orleans police and worked with the department on every aspect of the case.

"On behalf of my firm, I thank the New Orleans Police Department and Chief Bryant for their confidence in our firm. I would also like to thank Fontaine Barbeau for his complete support and help during the investigation."

Nick stepped away from the microphones.

"We will take a few questions," Chief Bryant said.

"Chief, is an arrangement like this unusual?" a reporter from WUPL-TV asked.

"Yes, in this case we thought this would be the best way to get leads on a multiple-victim case like this," the chief said.

The *Times Picayune* reporter asked, "What factor or factors were involved with you using Mr. Caldwell's firm?"

"They were on the ground, they had established a connection and Mr. Caldwell and his firm have an excellent record solving cold cases. Information about Mr. Caldwell and Mr. Cheswick and their staff will be available at the completion of this press conference," Chief Bryant said.

A young woman from WWL radio asked, "Mr. Caldwell, why does your firm focus on only cold cases?"

"Our firm doesn't just focus on cold cases. We do corporate and personal security, and we investigate theft and do background checks. Criminal and cold cases are investigated by one division of our firm," Nick said. "Most of those investigations, like this one, are conducted pro bono and we are funded by the firm and a foundation."

"What led you to pursue cold cases?" a reporter from the *Baton Rouge Advocate* asked.

"Those who no longer can advocate for themselves deserve justice as much as those who can," Nick said.

"That's all for now," Chief Bryant said. "As information becomes available that we can share, we will pass it on. Thank you for coming."

Other questions were shouted as Chief Bryant and Nick left the room.

"That wasn't so bad," Chief Bryant said.

"Speak for yourself," Nick replied.

Chief Bryant asked, "When are you taking off?"

"Some have left already, and most everyone else will leave tomorrow. I'm going to stick around and spend some time with Sinclair," Nick said. "As I said, if you need us for anything, we'll come back."

"It's been a pleasure working with you," Chief Bryant said.

Nick replied, "Likewise."

"I hope we'll see you soon," Chief Bryant said.

"You will, when you come up for that Bears game," Nick said.

They both laughed.

Chapter 56

Katie knocked on Nick's door. "Come on Pops we're burning daylight."

"Go away, and your John Wayne imitation sucks," Nick said.

"Come on. Casey, Phil and I are heading out soon and we want you there when we give Sinclair a surprise," Katie said.

"Video it. I can watch it later," Nick said.

"Get your butt out of bed, Pops, and get downstairs in five minutes, got it?" Katie said.

Nick mumbled to himself, "She's getting more like Mrs. Marbles and my sister every day," as he got out of bed and put on his robe and looked for his slippers. "Where the hell did the left one go?"

+

He entered Sinclair's office and saw Casey, Phil and Katie drinking coffee while Sinclair puffed away on his morning pipe.

"Good morning, starshine," Sinclair said, with more than the usual sarcasm.

"Well, good morning to you, old timer," Nick said.

"They have been running the clip from the press conference all morning," Sinclair said.

"It's easier than actually doing journalism," Nick said.

Katie asked if anyone needed anything. No one did. Ruby and Baron followed her out.

"Nick, what do you want to do with the St. Louis office?" Casey asked.

"Why don't we pay rent for a couple of more months," Nick said.

"Our lease isn't up until the end of January," Casey said.

219

"Perfect, I want to move," Nick said.

"You want to move? Do you know where?" Phil asked.

"I have a few ideas," Nick said. "Someplace more like the old office in the Loop."

"They going to open a Blackie's in St. Louis I haven't heard about?" Phil said with a laugh.

"How much room will we need?" Casey asked.

"Don't know, I have to think about it," Nick said. "Sinclair, if I decide to work out of St. Louis, are you in?"

"I might be if I can get T.R. to run the New Orleans' office and persuade Alex Hicks to intern," Sinclair said.

"What do you think, Phil?" Nick asked.

"Works for me," he said.

"What about you, Casey," Nick asked.

"It's a good idea," she said. "Are you giving up the office in Chicago?"

"No, but I think I'll spit my time between St. Louis and Chicago, and Sinclair can split his time between New Orleans and St. Louis," Nick said. "Is that okay with you, Sinclair?"

"Fine with me," he said.

Baron and Ruby cane from the kitchen with Katie, who was leading a large dog on a leash. She took the leash off and the dog walked over to Sinclair, hopped up on the couch with him and sat next to him.

"Who is this?" Sinclair asked.

Katie smiled. "This is Argo."

"Well, hello Argo. Who does he belong to?" Sinclair asked.

"He belongs to you," she said.

Sinclair said, "He looks old and ornery."

Katie smiled. "He is, he's a rescue dog."

"Who's he going to rescue?" Sinclair asked.

"You," Katie said.

"Perfect," Sinclair said. Argo looked at him and put his head in his lap and stretched out. Sinclair put his hand on Argo's head and stroked it. "I guess I'm going to have to take

220

him shopping for a collar and a bowl. I should probably get him some toys, too."

"Katie, you missed the conversation about St. Louis," Nick said.

"No, I knew you were considering it," she said.

"How did you know?" Nick asked.

"Mrs. Marbles told me," Katie said.

"How did she know?" Nick asked.

"Really?" she said.

"Her superpowers," Nick said.

Katie said, "Yep."

"So, what do you think?" Nick asked.

"I like St. Louis. I wouldn't mind working there," she said. "Have you decided yet?"

"Not yet," Nick said. "When I get back to Chicago, Bart and I will talk about it and make a decision. What time are you all heading out?"

"We need to get moving soon," Phil said.

"Who's going where?" Nick asked.

"We're all going back to Chicago," Casey said. "Then, I'll go back to St. Louis after we know what the plan going forward will be."

"What are you going to do?" Phil asked.

"I'm going to stay here for a few more days," Nick said, "if it's all right with Sinclair."

"Argo, is it okay with you if he stays?" Sinclair asked.

Argo lifted his head and yawned.

"Looks like he doesn't care one way or another," Sinclair said. "So, I guess it's all right.

"Thank you, Argo," Nick said.

+

Casey, Katie and Phil left for the airport after a tearful exit with Sinclair.

The house was quiet for the first time in several weeks. Nick and Sinclair, along with Argo, Baron and Ruby, sat in Sinclair's office.

"Do you want to talk about the case?" Nick asked.

"You did what we do, you got the bad guys," Sinclair said.

"You don't have any questions?" Nick asked.

"Maybe a few," Sinclair said.

"Ask," Nick said.

"Your confidential informant," Sinclair said.

"Yeah," Nick said.

"It wasn't just Alex Hicks, was it?" Sinclair asked.

Nick looked at Sinclair. "If I tell you, they won't be confidential informants anymore, will they?"

"Nick, cut the bullshit," Sinclair said.

"Sinclair..." Nick said.

"Nick..." Sinclair said

"Ask the question you want to ask," Nick said.

"Quit dancing around," Sinclair said, "was it Deidra?"

Nick looked down, then looked Sinclair in the eye. "It was."

They both sat in silence for a few minutes.

Sinclair said, "Then my dream was..."

"Was right on the money," Nick said. "You know, she is just like her old man, only prettier."

Sinclair smiled. "Do you think I'll ever see her again?" Sinclair asked.

"I wouldn't be surprised," Nick said. "Any other questions?"

"Yes, why are you leaving Chicago?" Sinclair asked, "and no bull."

"I love Chicago, but I need a change. I want to do what I do, like I used to.

"I'm happy with what Bart has done with the corporate division but that's not for me. I'm grateful that it gives us the funding we need to do the cold cases and the other kind of cases we did when we started, but I'll never be comfortable doing investigations for large companies or doing personal security gigs.

"I liked the old office. I liked working above Blackies. It was simpler, we took interesting cases, we helped folks. I'm a shamus, a gumshoe, at heart and always will be."

"Does Bart know how you feel about this?" Sinclair asked.

"He gets it, I have the greatest business partner anyone could have. He understands," Nick said. "He is very supportive and always has been, but as long as I'm in Chicago, I will feel obligated to be involved with the corporate side. We started the cold case foundation to create a separation between the two and it's not like the criminal investigation side doesn't make a profit. It does but not the kind of profit the corporate side makes."

Sinclair smiled. "I get it too."

Nick said, "If they need me on a case, I'll be there but…"

Sinclair said, "But you're still a cop at heart that requires more flexibility than a police department can allow."

Nick laughed. "Exactly, but don't ever say that in front of my dad or my brother."

"Your secret's safe with me," Sinclair said, with a smile. Go get cleaned up, we're going out to dinner with an old friend."

"T.R.?" Nick asked.

"Nope," Sinclair said, "we're having dinner with Fontaine Barbeau."

"With Fontaine?" Nick asked.

"We were close in the old days, and I blamed him after Deidra's death. It wasn't fair. He has lost a child now too and he needs a friend," Sinclair said.

"This is a side of you I haven't seen very often," Nick said.

"Don't get used to it." Sinclair laughed.

Chapter 57

Bags were packed and dog crates loaded into the car. Nick and Sinclair were having breakfast. While Argo was lounging next to Sinclair's chair, Ruby and Baron flanked Nick's chair.

"What route are you taking back?" Sinclair asked.

"I'm going to follow the Great River Road up I 55," Nick said. "I plan on stopping in Memphis to see a Red Bird game, then I am going to St. Louis and check the office and Laura and Bob's house, and I will try to catch a Gateway Grizzly game. Then head up to Springfield and spend a day at the Lincoln Museum, then head to Chicago. I should be back to Chicago by the end of the week. I told Bart I would be back in the office sometime Friday."

"Taking your time to get back, huh?" Sinclair said.

"I'm in no hurry," Nick said. "I want a little time to think."

"Call me from the road," Sinclair said.

"You worried about me?" Nick said, with a laugh.

"Not you, I worry about Baron and Ruby," Sinclair said. "Nick, thank you for what you did."

"No thank you needed. We just did what we do, catch bad guys, right," Nick said.

"That's what we do," Sinclair said.

"I'd better get on the road," Nick said.

They walked out on the front porch and shook hands. Nick, Baron and Ruby got in the car. Nick waved goodbye. As he drove off, he looked in the rearview mirror. He saw Sinclair and Argo and he wasn't sure, but he thought he saw someone else on the porch. He smiled.

Chapter 58

"You took your damned time getting back here," was the first thing Nick heard when he walked through the office door.

"I missed you too, Mrs. Marbles," Nick said.

Baron and Ruby ran to her, wagging tales and butts.

"I missed you two; have you been good puppies?" Mrs. Marbles asked, as she gave them treats.

Casey came out of an office. "Did you have a good trip back?"

"I did, I went to a couple ballgames and went to the Lincoln Museum," Nick said.

Nick's sister, Laura, walked out of his office. "Is our house still standing?"

"It is," Nick said. "Where is everybody?"

"Felix and Phil are at the corporate office and Katie and Alana will be in later," Casey said.

"Where's Cal and Greg?" Nick asked.

"They are at the at the safe house checking the equipment back in," Laura said.

"Is Bart up at corporate?" Nick asked.

"No," Mrs. Marbles said, "he is in his office waiting for you."

"Good," Nick said. He went to Bart's door and knocked.

"Come in," Bart said. Nick entered his office. "When did you start knocking?"

"What are you doing here today, slumming?" Nick said.

"I can see you're rested and back to your old self," Bart said, laughing.

"Why shouldn't I be?" Nick said.

"Well, after your supernatural experience, I thought you might be looking at things differently," Bart said.

"What supernatural experience would that be?" Nick asked.

"Really, Nick?" Bart said. "I see denial is not just a river in Africa."

"Bart, I hope you keep your day job because with a joke like that you will never make it as a standup," Nick said.

Bart laughed. "I guess we should get to it; let's talk about St. Louis. Are you sure that is what you want to do? You know I want you to stay here, you're my best friend and the idea that you won't be here is difficult for me."

"I know, but we talked about making a clear distinction between the corporate business and the foundation and the criminal work," Nick said.

"Yeah, I know, but I hoped you would want to run it out of this office," Bart said.

"I will split my time between Chicago and St. Louis. I spoke with Sinclair, and he is willing to split his time between St. Louis and New Orleans," Nick said.

"What's going to happen to the New Orleans office," Bart asked.

"He wants to bring T.R. into the New Orleans' office and he is going to try to get Alex Hicks in as an intern," Nick said.

"Who's going to the St. Louis office?" Bart asked.

"Casey and Phil are already there. Katie, Cal and Alana want to go and when Greg graduates, I think he would like to come down and split his time too," Nick said.

"What about Constance?" Bart asked.

"She wants to stay in Chicago and so do Bob and Laura," Nick said, "and Mrs. Marbles would stay here. The investigators that you have in corporate are not criminal investigators. All that I am saying is that we're just moving the criminal investigators."

"Okay, I just wish you could stay here," Bart said.

"I want to get out of Chicago," Nick said. "I need a fresh start."

"I respect that," Bart said. "I'm going to miss all of you."

"I know. I have questions. Are we able to support the St. Louis, New Orleans and this office? Nick asked.

"Yes, with the foundation funding and the revenue that the criminal investigations bring in," Bart said, "we're good. The corporate doesn't fund the criminal investigation division; it's self-sufficient. Every time we solve a high-profile case the corporate side gets ten to twenty inquiries from prospective clients. When do you want to make the move?"

"I want to take some time, probably a few months. Since Casey and Phil are already in the St. Louis office, they will go back and keep the office open," Nick said. "I want to have the time for the others to find a place to live and settle in. I am thinking trying to get everything in place by Fall."

"How many are in the St. Louis office now?" Bart asked.

"Since we were talking about closing the office last year, and Laura and Bob moved up here, we lost many of the investigators we had on staff," Nick said. "Now, the full-time staff is just Casey and Phil and part time we have Papadakis and a few old investigators that worked for the Crowley Agency before Big Jack retired."

"Let's do it," Bart said. "You're still going to be a Bears fan, right?"

Nick smiled. "For better and/or mostly worse."

Chapter 59

Nick spent the rest of the day in the Clark Street office working with Mrs. Marbles, Casey, and Phil discussing the move. They decided that the Clark Street office would be the main office for the Cold Case Foundation and serve as an office for the two Chicago investigators that they would hire. Mrs. Marbles would, of course, be in charge since she was the Executive Director of the Foundation. Greg would also work out of Clark Street until he graduated, and Bart said that it would be fine with him if Constance Treble wanted to work out of that office.

The St. Louis office would be the main office for the investigative branch, for the foundation and the criminal investigations. Nick would head the office and Casey would manage the office. Phil would be the lead investigator. Katie, Alana and Cal would be the investigative team.

When the meeting was over, Casey and Phil headed to Midway to catch a flight to St. Louis.

Chapter 60

Nick walked home a little after eleven. He changed clothes and took Baron and Ruby for a walk around Wrigleyville. They walked around Wrigley Field and looked at the statues of the Cubs greats. By the time they arrived back at the house Baron and Ruby were ready for bed.

Nick fixed himself a sandwich, poured himself a scotch, put the *Maltese Falcon* DVD in, and sat on the couch. Baron and Ruby joined him and fell asleep. As he watched the film his mind wandered back to New Orleans. He wondered if Deidra had visited Sinclair and how Fontaine was coping with what his son had done. He thought about Trip and hoped he would be a comfort to his grandfather. He hoped that all the women who had lost their chance for a full life because of a deranged zealot had found peace. He thought of the nineteen families that would have a piece of themselves missing forever.

He thought about the people and things he would miss in Chicago and wondered if he was trading one corrupt city for another. Chicago had changed over the last few years, as most cities were changing. Was anyone safe anymore? There seemed to be more bad guys than good guys.

Nick laughed. He thought if you were going to have a pity party, there was no better way than to have it alone with just your dogs to listen. He always did this kind of thing after a case, particularly after the cases that dealt with young people. He always got a little down after a case. Even when he solved a case, it didn't seem to be enough.

As Humphrey Bogart, a.k.a. Sam Spade, told Ward Bond, a.k.a. Det. Tom Polhaus, the Falcon was "the stuff that dreams are made of." Nick got up from the couch and got another scotch. He walked over to the front window, the street was dark and quiet, there was no traffic, no late-night walkers.

He started to turn away when he saw a light go on in an apartment across the street. He did a double take. The light was on in the apartment that Maureen Roberts had rented to stalk him. Her sister, Charlotte, had been shot and killed by Nick while she was trying to kill him. Maureen had vowed to kill Nick...when it was convenient for her.

Over the years, she continued to threaten to kill him, but at the same time they became "friendly." They liked to verbally spar with each other. She even helped solve an important case. After that case, as was her way, she disappeared.

He went to the lamp on the table in front of the window and turned it on. The window across the street went out. He shook his head and thought, this is crazy. He decided to go to bed.

He got Baron and Ruby up and went upstairs and got settled in bed, turned out the light and tried to fall asleep. He almost drifted off to sleep when the phone rang.

He picked it up and said, "What?"

"Hello, lover boy, miss me?"

"No," Nick said.

"Oh, Nickie, come on now, I know you missed me. I've missed you," she said, with a giggle.

"Maureen, what do you want?" he said.

"I was worried about you," she said.

"Worried about me? Why?" he said.

"There are a lot of reasons, lover boy," she said.

"Stop calling me that. By the way when are you going to kill me?" he said.

"Kill you?" she said. "I've told you before, I'm not going to kill you. I'm not even going to torture you, my darling. You do a much better job of that than I could ever do."

"Well, I won't disagree with you about that," he said. "Why did you call. I haven't heard from you in almost a year."

"I read about your New Orleans case," she said. "That was a good thing you did for Sinclair."

"It's what we do," Nick said.

"Nickie, you're beginning to sound like one of those books the professor writes about you," she said. "I liked the last book; he made me sound glamorous and mysterious."

"I thought he made you sound cunning and ruthless," Nick said.

"Oh, Nickie, you certainly know how to flatter and sweet talk a girl," Maureen said. "You know we are two sides of the same coin."

"Yeah, the bad penny that keeps showing up," he said.

"Nickie, you're just cranky and depressed; this always happens to you after you close a case. You just aren't happy unless you have bad guys to go after," she said. "I know lots of bad guys; I would be happy to point you in their direction and you could hunt them down, if you like."

"Thank you," Nick said, "but I can find my own cases."

"We could do it together; it would give us a chance to bond," she said. "Come on, Nick, your brother Wil absolved me of all the crimes you suspected me of."

"Maureen, he didn't absolve you, he just didn't arrest you, because you helped on the Crowe case," Nick said.

"Are you ever going to forgive me for threatening to kill you?" Maureen asked. "I forgave you for killing my sister."

"Maureen, I shot her after she shot me and tried to kill me, for God's sake," Nick said.

"Well, she didn't kill you. You are such a stickler about details, Nick, and that's why you aren't a happy person."

"Maureen, I have a lot to do in the morning, so I have to get some sleep," Nick said.

"We belong together, and you know it," she said. "This isn't the end, Nick."

"Maybe not, but it is the end for this part of the story," Nick said. "Good night, Maureen."

"Good night, lover boy," Maureen said.

Nick hung up. He opened the drawer of the nightstand next to his bed. He took his Glock out and put it on top of the nightstand to ensure a safe night's rest.

He thought better safe than dead.

As he drifted off to sleep, the phone rang. He didn't want to pick it up, but he did.

Nick didn't recognize the number. "Caldwell, I hope this is important."

"Mr. Caldwell, I don't know If you remember me, this is Johnny Crewson, you were a friend of my mother and father."

Johnny Crewson was the son of Randy and Kay Crewson, friends of Nick from high school. They had moved to St. Louis after college. His mother Kay committed suicide in front of Johnny and his younger brother Jimmy when they were nine and seven years old, twenty years ago.

Kay suffered from depression and reportedly paranoia.

"Johnny, how are you?"

"I've been better," Johnny said.

"What's going on, Johnny?" Nick asked.

"You do cold cases, don't you?" Johnny asked.

"I do. What's this about?" Nick asked

"I want you to investigate the murder of my mother," Johnny said.

"Johnny, your mom committed suicide. You know that," Nick said.

"She was murdered," Johnny said.

"Why do you say that?" Nick asked.

"She was not well, and she was driven to take her life," Johnny said.

"By whom?" Nick asked.

"By my dad and Sharon," Johnny said.

"You're saying your dad and your stepmother drove your mom to suicide?" Nick asked.

"Yes," Johnny said.

"How do you know that?" Nick asked.

"I know because I remember things my mom said. And there are others who remember what was going on back then," Johnny said.

"Johnny, this would be difficult to prove," Nick said.

"Mr. Caldwell, you remember she killed herself on their tenth anniversary," Johnny said, "the night of their anniversary party."

"I remember. I was there that evening," Nick said, "but what makes you think your dad and Sharon drove her to kill herself?"

"My dad and Sharon are moving to a new house." Johnny said.

"And?" Nick said. "While Jimmy and I were helping them pack we found her old trunk in the attic. It had her college yearbooks, her wedding dress and we found her diary and her last entry was the day she died," Johnny said. "She spelled out what she suspected, she was scared, and she was pushed over the edge."

"Johnny, why are you calling me?" Nick asked.

"When she died you were with the Chicago police," Johnny said.

"I was. I had only been with the department for a couple years," Nick said.

"I know, but she wrote in her diary that you told her that you wanted to be a detective," Johnny said.

"I don't remember that but most everyone I knew was aware that was my goal," Nick said.

"The last thing she wrote," Johnny said, "was, 'If anything ever happens to me call Nick, he'll find the truth.' So, I'm calling."

"Johnny, even if this were true, it would be impossible to get a criminal conviction," Nick said.

"I don't care about a conviction, I want the truth, I want dad and Sharon to be exposed for who and what they are. It will be the only way for Jimmy and me to get peace," Johnny said.

Nick was silent for a moment.

"Johnny, I will be coming to St. Louis in a few weeks to work out of our office there. When I get there, why don't you and Jimmy come in and we can talk," Nick said. "I can't promise anything, but I will listen to you and go over what information you have."

"Thank you, Mr. Caldwell," Johnny said.

"See you in a few weeks," Nick said, then hung up.

Nick rolled over and tried to go to sleep, but he couldn't stop thinking of Johnny. He wondered why when people say they want justice, it always sounds like they really want revenge.

The End

Biography

Deidra's Last Dance is Wm. Sharpe's eighth novel and the sixth in the Nick Caldwell series. He developed a love for the detective mystery which he calls *"neo noir pulp fiction."* As to why he calls it that, he has only said, he "likes how it sounds." He did say "that mysteries, thrillers, suspense, and imaginary fiction are guilty pleasures to have fun with and to escape from day-to-day hum drum and the nightly news. They are written to be enjoyed." He suggests when reading them you hide your copy inside a cover of *War and Peace*. You will enjoy your reading and make your friends believe that you are a serious intellectual.

He became interested in paperback mysteries because his father loved them. He began writing because his mother wrote a lot; unfortunately, she would never share her writing with the family. He explains that "Sometimes such is the way of Irish and Scottish families, 'controlled dysfunction.' We are born with a sense of sarcasm, humor and a wealth of stubbornness and crankiness."

Sharpe lives in Saint Louis, Missouri, with his wife Linda and Baron and Ruby, their ferocious BearhounDs. They enjoy visits from their son and daughter, Eric and Elise. Eric lives with his ferocious black cat Tinkerbell and Elise lives with her ferocious puppy Sheiky.

When not working on a story, he hunts for treasures in secondhand stores and he appears on two podcasts: *UnCommonSense Radio 4.0 the Podcast* with Lou Conrad, where his job is to be cranky, and with James Sodon on *Novel Approach*, a podcast about books and writing. He also watches anything that is streaming so he doesn't have to watch the news.

His day job is teaching, but most of the time now he spends staying indoors, washing his hands, trying to find the properly fitted mask and of course complaining loudly.

Books by Wm. Sharpe and James Sodon

Death by Lethal Affection
Justice Delayed
Uncle Joe is Dead
Not Forgotten
When Christmas Trees Flew
Dead Crowe
A Christmas Project
Deidra's Last Dance

* * *

Made in the USA
Monee, IL
11 June 2023

35479753R00134